"We've done it Annie." Her doubts vanished when she saw him there, looking at her as if she were a jewel beyond price.

Without further waste of time or words, she ran into his arms, all doubts and fears abandoned. She was kissed with a very satisfying violence. "I never thought . . ." he began to say, but was soon kissing her again, hungrily crushing her against him in a way that promised to harm his wound.

"Alex, do be careful," she cautioned in a breathless voice.

"I've been careful all my life, Duck. We have three lost years to make up. How soon can we start?"

Fawcett Crest Books
by Joan Smith:

A COUNTRY WOOING

Joan Smith

FAWCETT CREST • NEW YORK

A Fawcett Crest Book
Published by Ballantine Books
Copyright © 1987 by Joan Smith

Library of Congress Catalog Number: 86-91390

ISBN: 0-449-21087-1

Manufactured in the United States of America

First Edition: April 1987

Chapter One

Anne Wickfield sat with her mother at Rosedale on a fine morning in May, knotting a fringe for her white shawl, as though it were just any ordinary day and not the most exciting one in years for her—for the whole neighborhood. Lord Penholme had arrived home from the Peninsular War the evening before. The servants had been the first to hear it, word traveling via the domestic grapevine that exists in small country communities. He had been expected for some weeks now, and at last he had come.

Rosedale, the closest home to Penholme, would surely be the first to hear of his adventures in Spain and of his plans for the future. For centuries there had been more than physical proximity between the two houses. The families had fought side by side in the same battles, defending Charles I against Cromwell's Roundheads, and William and Mary against the Jacobites. Their sons and daughters had fought, played, worked, loved, and married together. They were so intertwined, they almost considered themselves one family.

"It will be good to have Alex back," Mrs. Wickfield said for about the third time that morning. The comment was not so innocent as it sounded. It was accompanied by a questioning glance at Anne, who failed to understand, or at least acknowledge, its full significance.

The existence of a bachelor at Penholme and a spinster at Rosedale quite naturally raised hopes of an attachment between them, but Anne felt the new lord would be looking for someone higher than a provincial cousin for his bride. The Penholmes had always been the more prestigious family, and Alex was ambitious. Three years before, he had left the Hall as plain Lord Alexander, determined to make his way in the world, for it was his elder brother, Charles, who had inherited the estate and title when their father had died.

"Yes, he'll have his hands full getting things back in shape, with Charles dead for eighteen months," Anne said, and calmly turned her shawl to begin fringing the last side.

"It was a blessing in disguise when he fell off his hunter and died," her mother said curtly. It had been a hard blessing for Anne, however, for she had been wildly fascinated with him. The feeling was not entirely mutual, though Charles had favored her with some flirtation when he was at home. "Between the old earl's extravagance and Charles's wanton ways, Penholme is run into the ground. But Alex is the one to take things in hand, as he did when his father died. Charles was too busy gallivanting. Alex was always the better manager. If it weren't for him, the whole family would be in the poorhouse."

Anne's face wore no condemning frown. She carried in her mind's eye an idealized memory of Charles. He had had all the devastating charm of the Penholmes, much more so than the present earl. Charles had been friendly, agreeable; he had thrown lavish balls at the Hall and taught the local ladies how to waltz. How could any girl with blood in her veins not have loved him? Alex was neither so tall, so handsome, nor quite so well loved, but he was the earl now, and his coming was awaited eagerly.

"I think it was shabby of Alex to run off and leave his brother short-handed. Charles depended on him to run the Hall. I daresay Charles would have settled down in time," Anne said tolerantly.

"He showed no sign of it in the five years he ruled the roost! The only difference between him and his father was that Charles was a bachelor and squandered his time and money in London half the year. Parties, horses, gambling! All the vices of the father, with an interest in women thrown in."

"There's no point raking up the past, Mama. He's dead."

"It's typical of Fate's contrariness that Alex should have caught a bullet the very week he got news of Charles's death. He must have been severely wounded, to have waited so long to come home."

Time, Anne felt, was relative. For five years she had waited, hoping Charles would "settle down," yet it hadn't seemed so long. She would have married him in a flash—wanton ways and all—if he'd offered. There had been seasons when this seemed possible. Indeed, the notion that he might yet come up to scratch had not entirely evaporated at the time of his death. He had hinted that financial affairs at the Hall made it necessary for him to marry an heiress, but she had figured that was his gentlemanly way of damping her ardor, as no heiress had ever been brought home. She certainly regretted losing Charles but, unlike her mother, saw no likelihood of attaching Alex, nor much inclination for it either. It was not the countess's tiara that had drawn her to the late Lord Penholme.

Not that she disliked Alex. She really didn't know him

3

as well as the other members of the family. From having loved Charles for so long, she knew him very well. Robin, nearly her own age, was as familiar to her as a brother, and as dear. The youngsters she saw nearly every day when they weren't having lessons, and the eldest sister, Rosalie, had been such a beauty that everyone knew her. The expectation that she would make a grand match had been filled to the full. A duke, no less—the Duke of Exmore. But Alex. . . .

How had it come she knew so little of him? He'd been the quiet one of that rambunctious family, a little aloof. Even a quiet Penholme, however, was not a quiet person. You couldn't say Alex was shy. He was popular, had his own friends, but he had been overshadowed by Charles. Very likely that accounted for his manner. A younger son would lack the assurance and self-confidence of the eldest. Alex hadn't counted for much while Charles had been alive. It had always been of his eldest and favorite son that the old earl spoke, and always Charles that the girls had chased after. The countess used to be fonder of Alex than the others, Anne thought. And the countess had died six years before in childbirth. The Penholmes were extravagant in everything, even the size of their family. Ten of them born, two dying in infancy, Charles now dead, and Rosalie married. Still six of them at home, including Alex. And four of them were young enough to require a mother.

Alex, the manager, would no doubt manage that as well, in short order. He'd choose some lady whose dowry would set Penholme to rights and provide a mother for his ready-made brood in the bargain.

Anne supposed it must have been a difficult time for Alex when his mother died, then his father the next year— from a broken heart, really, though his death certificate said pneumonia. The old earl was no philanderer, whatever his other faults. It was expected that Alex would move to Sawburne, the small estate his father had purchased, reputedly for his second son, but it hadn't happened. Instead, he'd managed Penholme for Charles, till he suddenly decided to make his career in the army.

"I wonder why Alex ever went to Spain," Anne said musingly.

"Lots of younger sons do," her mother answered.

"He was always . . . strange," Anne said for lack of a better word. "I mean, he never dropped in on us unannounced, the way the others did. He never took potluck with us or joined us as a matter of course when we met in the village. Even Rosalie always did that, and you know Rosalie, . . ."

"A mighty high instep, but of course a well-turned one. Too pretty for her own good, that one."

"You know, as I think about it, I don't believe Alex ever came to this house without a reason," Anne continued. "He used to deliver the rabbits or pheasants Charles had sent, but he'd leave as soon as he said good morning. He never stayed to chat or for a cup of tea, and you know how all the Penholmes love their tea."

"From the day they were weaned from their wet nurse. But Alex attended all the family parties. I've seen you stand up with him at the assemblies and balls, Anne, and a handsome couple you made."

Anne gave an impatient *tsk*. "Don't get that idea in your head, Mama. Rosalie will find him an heiress in London. Alex never cared for me in the least, and truth to tell, I was never particularly fond of him."

"Things change" was all her mother said, but her voice burdened the words with significance. She meant Charles was dead and Anne was twenty-two years old, with no sign

5

of a suitor on the horizon. Perhaps she meant even more than that. Rosedale would be Anne's home until her mother's death, when it would revert to Florian Wickfield. Not that Mama, at two and forty, was in imminent danger of demise.

Mrs. Wickfield spoke on to make her point perfectly clear. "Alex is no honeybee, like Charles, buzzing from lady to lady. When he singles out someone for his attention, she can be sure of marrying him, and he won't wait long, now that he's home. Twenty-seven is the right age for settling down. An excellent *parti*, dear. There's Penholme Hall, with an income of ten thousand a year, and Sawburne—the old lord paid ten for it. His wife made him buy it when he inherited money from his uncle, to keep him from gambling it away. There's the London house, and the hunting box in Leicester, worth a few thousand."

"The Hall is mortgaged, and besides, Sawburne will go to Robin when he marries. Don't be thinking Alex will settle for my fiddling dowry of five thousand."

"You'd be a good manageress and a fine mother for the children, Anne" was her mother's trump card, played last. "Alex will bear that in mind when he chooses." Mrs. Wickfield looked hopefully at her daughter to gauge the effect of her statement.

"He has Aunt Tannie to look after the children."

"That Cassandra! She's like a black cloud hovering over everything. I always feel I ought to be striking my breast and saying *mea culpa* when she starts her litany of complaints. And she's no manager, either. You and I have become pretty good managers, since the price of everything has gone up with this war. We make our own clothes."

"I've even turned cobbler," Anne said, failing to recognize a trump when she heard it. "I got out the hammer and last and nailed the loose sole back on my slipper today. The nails come through the insole and hurt like the deuce. I put some cotton wool in the toe." She smiled to think what Charles would say if he knew to what shifts she was sunk. Charles—she must forget Charles. Break that foolish habit she'd gotten into of harping on his memory, turning him into a paragon, now that he was dead. Really, a dead Charles was more lovable than a living one. Memory selected the endearing qualities and softened the pain of his less admirable traits—in particular his way of oiling around all the local girls.

"I'll make sure the kettle's boiling for tea. He should be here soon," Mrs. Wickfield said, and left, to give her advice time to do its work.

Anne's mind turned to Alex, but it did not flow along those lines suggested by her mother. She wondered if he'd come in his uniform. No, he wasn't the sort to strut and preen about in it. She'd never even seen him in his regimentals, though he'd sent Aunt Tannie a painting of himself so outfitted. He looked very good, too. Wide, straight shoulders and a soldier's stiff posture. The ladies would adore him in it.

Alex would more likely come posting down the lane in his hunting jacket and buckskins, probably carrying a rabbit for their dinner over his saddle. He wouldn't stay more than half an hour, even on this special day.

Glancing once again to the window, Anne saw a handsome bay mare trotting along. The man astride it wore a scarlet tunic, and as he drew nearer, she recognized the lineaments of Alex, who she must remember to call Penholme. A familiar pain stabbed her heart, to think that Charles was dead. She stared as Alex rode closer, till even his expression was visible. She saw no smile of

7

anticipation. He was just doing his duty. He looked thin, almost haggard, and wore a thoughtful frown.

But still he was home after three years, and she ran excitedly into the hall. "Mama! Mama, he's come!"

Chapter Two

Mrs. Wickfield was on thorns to see Alex. It would have seemed odd, had anyone been watching, that she slipped quietly up the servants' stairs to her room upon hearing Anne's call. The explanation for this bizarre behavior was that she hoped their first meeting might call forth some felicitous emotion, and they must be allowed privacy to indulge it. She had noted with satisfaction that Anne wore her best afternoon gown for the occasion, her blue mulled muslin, which matched her eyes and showed off her neat figure. As she wore the blue slippers that hurt her toe, she obviously wanted to appear at her best. Her brown curls might have been more festively arranged, but that was no matter. Anne's beauty was of the quiet sort that grew gradually upon the viewer. She never bowled a gentleman over at first meeting.

Mrs. Wickfield could not observe, of course, that Anne ran to the saloon door to greet Alex, her blue eyes sparkling and her cheeks as rosy as a young girl's from excitement, and a touch of self-consciousness due to her mother's hints. Alex was advancing quickly himself; they nearly collided at the doorway, causing them both to come to an abrupt halt. They stood a moment, staring silently. Then

Alex's smile broke, and he said in a husky voice, "Come and make me welcome as you were going to, Annie."

She took the last step into his arms and was folded in a surprisingly strong bear hug, an action that was totally unlike Alex. His cheek brushed hers. It felt warm and smooth. A tang of spice hung about him, perhaps from shaving lotion. She felt a little uneasy at this prolonged intimacy. She could even feel his breath on her cheek and the thud of his heart against her breast. It darted into her head that she had had no more intention of throwing herself into his arms than she had of striking him. Both seemed equally strange. Where had he gotten that idea?

She pulled back and looked at him. The first thing noticed was the regimentals; it's not easy to ignore a well-set-up gentleman, less than a foot from you, in a blazing scarlet tunic embellished with gold lace and brass buttons. The next thing was his face. It had changed. At first she thought it was the close-cropped brown hair that made him look different—older—but closer scrutiny told her it was his cheeks. They were leaner than before, and weathered to tan from Spain's sunny climate. Then she looked at his eyes and revised her opinion once more. It was the eyes that had changed. They were the same warm brown she remembered, but now they were set deeper in his thin face. The corners of them were etched with fine lines, giving him a somewhat hard look. But no, the glow in them was not hard; it was only startlingly intense.

"Oh, you've changed so, Alex!" she exclaimed even before she said "Welcome home."

"At the Hall they're calling me the walking skeleton"— he laughed nervously—"but Pembers will soon get me filled out. *You* haven't. Changed, I mean," he said, and his laughter changed to a peculiar smile. "Still the prettiest sight in the county," he said softly.

This, too, was unlike Alex. It almost had a touch of Charles about it. "Do you like my uniform?" he asked, turning to allow her to admire it from all angles. "I thought you might like to have a look before it's done up in camphor for posterity—or future costume balls."

"Very handsome! You'll be turning all the girls' heads if you go on the strut in it."

"I wouldn't want to go breaking every heart in the neighborhood, but I did want *you* to see it."

Had she imagined the inflection on "you"? She looked away, confused, and said, "Mama will want to see it, too. Where can she be? I called her. . . ."

His reply, though he was unaware of it, showed knowledge of his new importance. "The servants will tell her I'm here."

Every word that came out of his mouth surprised her. His coming in uniform surprised her, as did his saying fairly baldly that he wanted her to admire him. "Come in and sit down, Alex—Penholme!" she corrected herself, then looked uncertain, for though Alex had certainly donned his new dignity and title, has manner was freer than before.

"Penholme? Good God, you sound as though I'm a stranger. I haven't been gone that long, have I?"

"No, of course not. I—I didn't say welcome home, did I?" she asked in a little confusion.

"No, you didn't say you'd missed me either. I missed you," he added with a long, meaningful look into her eyes.

"Of course I missed you. We all did."

That blanket addition caused his smile to dwindle. "It's wonderful to be back. Shall we go in and have some tea?"

"Yes, certainly."

She led him into the saloon, uncomfortable under his close scrutiny. "How did you find the children? Very grown-up, I expect."

"I hardly recognized them, Youngsters change so quickly."

"You must have been shocked to hear of Charles's death," she said, for it seemed a subject that must be touched on.

Something in him froze. Her first impression that he had hardened was revived, and strengthened. "It was a shock to us all; but I lost many good friends in Spain. Death isn't the stranger—the tragedy—to me that it must have been for you, though, of course, losing a brother is different—worse."

She cast a wary eye on him. Charles's death had been a mixed tragedy for Alex, throwing him into his new position of power and prestige, which he was obviously enjoying.

Mrs. Wickfield, no longer able to contain her curiosity, came pelting downstairs to make Alex welcome. She saw none of that joyful reunion she'd been hoping and scheming for. Alex was as backward as ever, and Anne did nothing to set him at his ease. He had to rise again and show off his uniform and have his new slenderness exclaimed over.

"You still cut a gallant figure. Quite a pineapple of perfection in your red jacket. How is your shoulder, Alex? Not bothering you too much, I hope," she said solicitously.

"It's not bad now," he assured her.

Under Mrs. Wickfield's skillful encouragement, Alex stayed for an hour, nibbling macaroons, sipping tea, and regaling the ladies with humorous anecdotes of his military career in a fashion so unlike him as to make them wonder whether the sun had not turned his brain. Even an invitation to lunch was accepted, with a casual "I mentioned at the Hall I might be staying."

The combined minds of the Wickfield ladies had not

foreseen this degree of condescension, and it was to only an inferior luncheon that the returned hero sat down. At table, the conversation turned from the war to domestic matters. Alex had not discussed affairs with the bailiff or his man of business, had not ridden over his estate nor attended to any of the multitude of matters awaiting his attention.

"You'll have plenty to keep you hopping," Mrs. Wickfield warned him.

"At least there'll be no impediment to my doing what has to be done," he said curtly. Anne gave him a narrow-eyed glance, recognizing in the speech a slur against Charles. Even if it were true, she didn't feel he ought to have said it.

"I wonder you ever left, Alex, since you pretty well had control of the estate for Charles when you enlisted," she said.

"I had only responsibility, not authority. Now that I've enjoyed both, I realize the impossibility of that situation."

"I shouldn't think Charles would have been an unduly hard taskmaster," she said rather testily.

Mrs. Wickfield threw herself into the breach. "You'll have a trip to London and Sawburne as well, to take matters in hand there," she said.

"I mean to turn Sawburne over to Robin fairly soon. My father bought it with the second son in mind."

"Charles never gave it to you," Mrs. Wickfield said, nodding her head in approval of what she had heard.

"He would hardly do so when Alex was leaving for Spain," Anne pointed out.

"Why, Alex was here for two years, and . . ." Mrs. Wickfield became aware of a tension in the atmosphere and let her speech peter out to silence.

"Charles didn't intend to deprive me of it," Alex said,

but coldly, as one doing his duty. "He mentioned my having the use of it. I don't approve of the system of primogeniture we follow in England. If a man has five sons, as my father had, he ought to make some provisions for them all, and not give the lot to the eldest. It's foolishness to give one man so much consequence and put the others at his mercy, or the mercy of their own wits. Of course, I don't have anything equal to Sawburne to give Willie and Bung, but I'll do all in my power to see them started in some profitable career, or try to help them set up a place of their own if that's what they want."

Anne interpreted this to mean he'd make a good marriage. How else did he plan to have all this beneficence to distribute? Her mother said, "Why, Willie and Bung both want to be soldiers, like you. You won't have to do any more than buy them a commission."

"Boys of twelve don't know what they want. They think it's all parades and playing with guns. It's not like that, I promise you," he said grimly. "I'll give them a truer idea of what a soldier's life is like."

Willie and Bung were twins, so much alike that their own family had trouble telling them apart. Recently Bung had knocked a chip off the corner of his front tooth. It would not have bothered him a whit if only Willie could have done the same, but till they managed to get an identical chip off Willie's, their favorite stunt of posing as each other was ruined.

"When do you plan to turn Sawburne over to Robin?" Anne asked. "We shall miss him when he goes."

Alex looked alert at this question and in fact didn't answer it. "It's only five miles away. Not too far a distance to travel, if he has some special reason. Has he?" Anne and Mrs. Wickfield blinked a question at each other. Alex's voice was suddenly thin and cold as ice. "Is he seeing some local lady? He didn't tell me so. I hope she's not ineligible.''

"Oh, no!'' Anne said. "Good gracious, he's only twenty-one, Alex. A bit young to shackle himself for life.'' She noted, but didn't mention, the word "ineligible.'' It seemed Alex's ambitions extended to the whole family.

"Won't you need Robin to help you at Penholme?'' Mrs. Wickfield asked. "It's been a long time without a master. Robin and Mrs. Tannie do the best they can, but that last crew of bucks Charlie had staying there made a sorry shambles of the place. Shot off their pistols in the armaments room, and the south wall is still full of holes. One of them set fire to his room—the blue suite had its carpets burned. A set of black rags hang at the windows to this day. You'll need an extra man for the farms. And for the Hall itself, what you need is a wife, my lad,'' she said firmly, but was subtle enough not to glance at her daughter.

"Carpets and draperies won't take much mending,'' Alex answered. "It's the home farm and the tenant farms I'm worried about. I haven't had a look around yet. I know the man I hired for Charles before I left didn't stay long. I understand a Pat Buckram is acting as bailiff nowadays. Robin was overseeing things as best he could, but he's still green. I shan't send him to Sawburne till he's dry behind the ears.''

"It's a good thing you're back,'' Mrs. Wickfield declared, and seemed in much of a mind to go on disparaging Charles, till Anne stopped her.

"There's no need to go into all that, Mama. What's done is done.''

"Best not to speak ill of the dead, so I'll say no more about it,'' her mother agreed. Alex sat like a jug, not condemning but not saying a word in Charles's defense. "I can just imagine the excitement at the Hall when you arrived last night, Alex. Willie and Bung have lived at the roadside for three days. Set up a little tent with a flag on top and didn't stir from it from morning till night, so as to see you come home.''

"They nearly pulled me bodily from the gig when they recognized me. I borrowed the gig from the inn in Winchester, for I took the post down from London. They were disappointed I didn't arrive at the head of an army, or at least mounted on a steed. I had no cattle or carriage in London and didn't want to buy any till I got home and saw what was in the stable.''

"That was sensible." Mrs. Wickfield nodded and thought to herself that it was not the way Charles would have arrived. He'd have brought the flashiest nag he could find and hired an army to come after him.

"I shouldn't think you'd have to buy any horses or carriages," Anne said. "Robin is always complaining of the number of mounts in the stable. There seem to be plenty of carriages for everything.''

"I was amazed to see an even two dozen nags, with only the twins and Robin riding. And with all that horseflesh, there's nothing for the girls to ride. I must get a pair of ponies for Loo and Babe. Do you still ride, Anne?''

"Yes, still the same horse. Mrs. Dobbin is approaching my age, twenty-two, and is about ready for pasture.''

"What she's ready for is the glue factory," Mrs. Wickfield declared.

"Lord, are you still coaxing that old nag along the roads?" Alex exclaimed. "Why don't you get yourself a real mount?''

"Mounts cost money. We aren't the Penholmes, you know, to be throwing it around as though it were hayseed.''

Alex stared in surprise. "Surely you can afford a decent mount."

"Of course we could—if we thought it took precedence over having food on the table." Alex gave a guilty look at his plate, and she laughed. "No, really, we are not quite so hard up we begrudge you your mutton."

"You've no idea what's happened to money, Alex," Mrs. Wickfield said. "They blame it on the war, but it's the merchants filling their pockets, if you ask me. Mrs. Perkins—from the general store, you know—has set herself up a carriage and team, and she need not bother letting on she isn't putting half the increased price in her pocket. You have only to look at the Anglins—retired merchants from London, and millionaires. They've built a castle to rival Penholme. We who are living on a fixed income must make and mend as we can. We are getting pretty good at mending. Anne even took the hammer to her own slipper yesterday, to save paying the cobbler."

Alex laughed, thinking it a joke, but was soon told otherwise. "It's no laughing matter!" Mrs. Wickfield scolded him. "We used to be able to afford a trip to Bath or London once in a while, but with what money is worth today, we're lucky we can keep a gig to drive to Eastleigh."

A frown settled on Alex's brow as he listened. "Is it really that bad? Aunt Tannie has been reading me a list of woes, but I confess I paid her little heed."

"You'll see for yourself," Mrs. Wickfield continued, happy to air her grievance to a new audience. "Servants' wages are so high I threaten to turn maid myself. With the merchants able to offer them a fortune, we must do likewise or scrub our own floors. Our maid demands thirty-five pounds a year, if you please. We decided between us, Annie and I, that for that sum we could well make our own beds and run a dust cloth over the furniture."

"You have only the butler and cook, then?"

"Butler?" Mrs. Wickfield stared. "Nobody but lords and merchants has a butler. We have cook and a backhouse boy, who looks after the stable and does a bit of gardening and tends the fire. Just a boy, you see, so we don't have to pay the tax on him. He's ignorant as a whelp. Annie is teaching him to read and cipher. We pay him fifteen a year, and like him a deal better than Mary, for she turned into such a flirt, there was no standing it. She's gone up to Penholme to distract your footmen there and keep them from their chores. I told Aunt Tannie the girl is useless and certainly not needed at the Hall, but it went through her like a dose of salts. Charles hired a dozen girls after you left. Of course, the local girls do look to the Hall for work."

"Yes," Alex said doubtfully. "I thought there was an unconscionable crowd of servants hustling around, but I supposed they were all coming out of the woodwork to get a look at me."

"So they were, I expect," Mrs. Wickfield agreed. She found nothing unusual in the remark, but to Anne it sounded again unlike Alex. Some new consequence had come to him as a result of his inheritance, or perhaps it was the effect of the army. It would never have occurred to Lord Alex that the girls were coming forth to admire him. Her thoughts were turned from this by Alex's next statement.

"We're having a party at the Hall this evening in honor of my return. Just a small party—my family and you, if you will do us the honor."

Enthusiastic acceptances were given, and very soon Alex rose to take his leave. Mrs. Wickfield disappeared again, leaving Anne to show him the door. When he opened it, sunlight streamed in on them, throwing his lean cheeks into

18

shadow and accentuating the lines from his nose to his lips. He reminded her of the carvings of saints and martyrs seen in churches. There was an austere look about him. The war must have been horrid.

"Are things really as bad as your mother indicated?" he asked.

"We've never gone to bed hungry. I think *you* have, Alex."

"War is . . . different. I hadn't thought things would be so desperate at home."

"Hardly desperate. I hope you will tell me all about Spain sometime. I'm sure you had more dangerous adventures than stealing donkeys and hiding yourself in a flour bag."

"I plan to forget all that. This is a new beginning for . . . me."

There was a little hesitation before that last word. The intent, conscious beam in his eyes suggested a different word. "A new beginning for *us*" would have given a more suitable reading. Then he smiled, squeezed her fingers, said, *"Hasta mañana, querida,"* and left.

She laughed in surprise to hear an old friend suddenly crop out into a new language. "What does that mean?" she called after him. The words, though totally unintelligible, had an alluring sound.

"It means I'm very glad to be back. Very glad, Annie."

She closed the door and turned to see her mother hovering at the bottom of the stairs. "He's changed, don't you think?" Anne asked pensively.

"I'm glad to see he's come out of himself a little. He didn't use to stay to lunch. I half wish he hadn't taken it into his head to do it today. An omelette and cold cuts, and he looking as though he could eat a horse. We'll do better next time."

"If there is a next time. This may have been his ceremonial call."

"He'll be back. Alex won't waste much time to find a mother for the children and a proper mistress for the Hall. You'll have to look sharp and move fast to nab him. At least he never was one for throwing his cap at all the girls."

"But he's changed. You must have noticed, Mama. All that talk about people wanting to 'get a look at him.' He's very much aware of his worth."

"The man's not an idiot. Nor is he the type to be running to London to marry an heiress. You have the inner track, having known him forever."

But Anne didn't feel she knew him at all. What sparse knowledge she'd ever had of Lord Alex hardly seemed to apply to Lord Penholme. He was an intriguing stranger, and even spoke a new language. Travel was broadening, folks said, and it had changed Alex in some undefinable way. He looked harsher, more self-assured. He showed a latent anger toward Charles that she had not seen before he left. This annoyed her, but other thoughts soon pushed it from her mind. Something in this new old friend made her very much aware of herself as a woman. She remembered that long hug when he had arrived and the soft beam in his eyes when he had taken his leave in Spanish.

She shook away these vague thoughts. "You sound mighty eager to be rid of me, you unnatural mother," she joked.

"I'm only forty-two. Maybe I'd like to see you settled to try my hand at a beau."

"The butcher has been giving us the best cuts in the shop for a year now. I think you might have him if you played your cards right."

"It's not the butcher I have in mind. We owe the draper more, and he, of course, is a very fine gentleman. He hardly

20

ever spits on the floor like the butcher, and he has a charming flat over his shop. I would make a suitable Mrs. Mumbleton, don't you think?''

"Unexceptionable," Anne agreed blandly. "Then I could afford that piece of white crepe I've been eyeing this past month, for I shall expect a good family discount once you are keeping shop, Mama."

She thought of the white crepe with a wistful longing. How elegant she would look if she could wear it to Penholme Hall for this evening's family party. She pulled herself up short on the thought, for it wasn't Robbie or Aunt Tannie or the children she pictured admiring her. It was Alex.

Chapter Three

The ladies from Rosedale owned a carriage, but for the past six weeks it had sat in the stable, awaiting a new wheel. Unless a trip could be made in a gig, they remained at home. They often went to the Hall in the gig, and were surprised to see a carriage drive up to their door. Alex had sent Lord Robin to fetch them. It was not Robin's jet-black hair or his blue eyes and long lashes nor even his resemblance to the late Charles that made him a favorite with Anne. Having known him from the cradle, she was heedless of his appearance as he was himself. She valued him for his undemanding good nature, which was always happy to accommodate itself to circumstances.

"Hello, Aunt Alice, Annie." He smiled. Mrs. Wickfield was in fact his second cousin, but everyone from the Hall called her Auntie. "Alex has taken the cork-brained notion you'll freeze to death driving home in the gig, and sent me down for you."

"Cold in May? I cannot think so," Anne said, laughing.

"No more than can I," Robin agreed. "I daresay Alex finds anything below a hundred cold, after frying in Spain. Dark as a blackamoor, ain't he? And skinny as a rail."

Robin's unseeing eyes ran over Anne's best rose silk

gown without approval or the opposite. She picked up her white shawl, its fringe completed, and was ready for the trip.

The change of carriage was agreeable to Mrs. Wickfield, who preferred a closed vehicle after dark. "How did Alex know our carriage had fallen apart?" she asked.

"He must have been to the stable this morning, I suppose. He has eyes like a lynx, especially for things gone to ruin. I didn't realize the Hall was such a shambles, till he began lamenting. Have you heard the news?"

He didn't wait for an answer but rushed on with his announcement. "He's going to give me Sawburne. We're riding over soon to have a look around. Lord, I nearly fell over in shock when he told me. I made sure he'd drag his heels, as Charlie did when Papa died. I am to leave as soon as I learn how to command the whole fort by myself. He means to take the reins," he added, suiting the metaphor to his own preference.

"How soon?" Anne asked.

"A few months, as soon as we've become reacquainted and set Penholme to rights. I shall be lonely as a lobster. I'd like to take Willie and Bung with me, but they'd never leave the hero. Of course, Alex will be over often to steer me straight. I can learn a lot from Alex. He knows more about farming than any of us. He's been going over accounts with his man of business all afternoon and is dismal as dust about the mess things are in. Poor Buckram has had his ears singed so often they're smoking. My own are feeling hot. It seems Buckram is a bit of a *bandido*. However, I wrote Alex that we were going to rack and ruin, so I guess he ain't too surprised."

"I hope he gets the black curtains in the blue suite fixed up," Mrs. Wickfield said.

"No, sir, it's the tenant farms he's all het up about.

23

They haven't been bringing in anything like they should. He was nagging Charlie to do tiling and fencing and I don't know what-all before he left, but he never could get him to spend a sou on repairs, and the things still haven't been done. Now the actual houses are caving in besides—something about water seeping into the foundations. I daresay it will cost a monkey to fix. Sawburne's as dry as a board," he added complacently.

This sort of talk occupied them till they reached Penholme. It was like entering a second home, and a more attractive one than they left, entering the gold saloon at Penholme. The ravages of time and neglect were not so apparent in this front room. Golden draperies were less susceptible to discoloring than some shades, and the timeless Oriental carpets wore well. Aunt Tannie had ordered that the girls polish the fine old furnishings, and the oil paintings on the wall were still magnificent. The upholstered pieces were past their prime, but with so many people occupying them, their condition was seldom apparent.

The children were all allowed to stay up and take part in this happy family occasion. Willie and Bung were decked out in a pair of blue suits that showed an inch of wrist below the sleeves. They darted to the doorway to welcome their cousins in a raucous manner that threatened everyone's eardrums.

"Alex brought us real guns from Spain!" one of the twins shouted. It was impossible to tell which, as he kept his teeth hidden.

"Mine killed seven Frenchies!" the other boasted, well pleased with such an accomplished weapon.

"And a French flag with blood on it!" Bung said. A broad smile revealed his chipped tooth.

"How nice," Anne said. "I hope it is French blood."

Alex strolled up to greet the company. Anne noticed he had removed his uniform. His black jacket made him look more familiar than on his visit to Rosedale. But as he stood, gazing intently at her with a little smile curving his lips, she again had that odd sensation of looking at a stranger.

"Quit pestering your cousins," he chided the children.

Mrs. Wickfield went forward to receive a welcoming embrace. "Skin and bones," she complained, shaking her head at him. She tugged at his loose jacket. "You'll have to get yourself some new jackets, Alex."

"Not only myself. I'm ashamed to be seen in church with these two scarecrows," he said, tousling Bung's hair. "I can't believe how they've grown."

"We've growed six inches since you left," Willie boasted.

"You've growed illiterate, too," Alex said, leading them all into the saloon. "I notice the biggest change in Babe." He turned to the baby of the family as he spoke. Babe's hair was nearly blond, and arranged in a mop of natural curls that framed a pretty face. "She was only a tot when I left. Now she tells me she's reading, if you please." At that moment, she sat holding a large stuffed doll on her lap and ignoring the visitors.

Loo came forward, a plainer child but with promise of growing into a handsome young lady. "I'm all finished reading, and I'm writing," she informed the guests. Then as an afterthought she dropped a curtsy.

"I didn't see you writing me any letters, you minx," Alex said, and chucked her chin.

He couldn't seem to get enough of looking at them, of touching them. Loo put her hand in his and swung on it. "I would have wrote if I'd known you wanted me to," she apologized.

25

"Another illiterate. I thought you girls had a governess."

"Yes, she reads all the time," Loo told him. "She reads novels. She's reading me all about a haunted house in Cornwall, with a dungeon and a ghost."

"Edifying!" Alex said, lifting a brow. "We must look into this novel-reading governess and see if she ever reads grammar. Come and sit down, ladies, if you can find a chair for this brood of gypsies cluttering up the place."

It was not impossible to find two more seats in a room that boasted six sofas and a dozen chairs, but it was impossible to find any silence or privacy. The children still found their soldier brother too marvelous a novelty to leave his side, and he didn't seem much disposed to pushing them off. He took Babe on his knee and put up with the twins' pestering in a very good spirit.

"Why did you take off your uniform, Alex?" Bung demanded.

"Because I've already showed it off."

"I wish I had a uniform like yours," Willie said. "I'd go and shoot a million Frenchies."

"Do you think I wore that nice outfit to crawl through the mud and kill my fellowman? That one's reserved for slaying ladies."

"Did you bring your fighting outfit home? Can I see it, Alex?"

"I didn't carry a tattered, mud-stained coat home. I never want to see it again."

"I wish *I* had it. I'd love to have it," Bung declared.

"It was full of lice," Alex said blandly.

Bung stared, disbelieving. "Lice! In your clothes?"

"Certainly. It's not easy to bathe when you're bivouacking in a field."

Mrs. Tannie shook her head sadly. "You're making my

26

flesh creep, Alex. I can feel vermin crawling all over me. And you, Master Jackanapes," she added to Robin, "never mind peering at me like a stuffed frog. Lice should not be discussed in company."

From long familiarity with her dark humor, the family had learned to ignore Aunt Tannie.

"What did you eat?" Willie asked.

"Whatever we could find. A rabbit, if we were lucky. Roots, windfall oranges, bitter as bedamned. Black bread. How I look forward to Pembers's dinner. And sleeping in a bed with no rats prowling around, no rain falling on me, no fear of a bullet parting my hair."

The twins exchanged a wary look. Anne assumed their brother's propaganda of disillusionment had begun.

"The fighting and shooting must have been exciting," Willie suggested hopefully.

"Very exciting. Of course, not many days are actually spent fighting and shooting. The dreariest part of being a soldier is the waiting. Sitting around for a month, waiting to attack. Then a day's 'fighting and shooting,' as you call it. The survivors who aren't maimed ride twenty miles and wait another month."

Willie frowned into his lap. He lifted his head and smiled. "I'll bet it'd be exciting being a sailor!"

"A pity we couldn't ask Admiral Lord Nelson," Alex said. "Of course, he's been shot dead already, after losing one eye and one arm. But I daresay it would be great fun."

Willie was displeased with his hero. "Charlie always said you were having the best time of any of us. He wished *he* was free to go off to war, but he had responsibilities."

Anne stole a look at Alex, expecting some show of anger. She was surprised to see only sadness. "He remembered it occasionally, did he?'' The words stung her, but she was still surprised at the sad spirit behind them.

"Alex, didn't you *like* being a soldier?" Bung asked.

"I liked parts of it well enough. It wasn't what I thought it would be when I joined up. I didn't know the uniforms got so dirty, Bung, and so full of holes.''

"Bullet holes?" Bung asked, ever the optimist.

"We'll talk about it later—it's impolite to bore our guests.''

The guests had shown no signs of boredom, but Babe and Loo had to tell their cousins what souvenirs had been brought home for them. The showing of Loo's mantilla and Babe's Spanish doll proved a genteel diversion in the conversation.

"I got you two ladies a souvenir as well," Alex said, but he didn't present the gifts yet, and soon Aunt Tannie bustled them in to dinner.

"I hope the pork isn't burned to a cinder,'' she scolded. "The grease from it has been smoking up the place for hours. Not that one can blame Pembers, with the stove he has to work with. We need a new stove, Alex.''

The pork was delicious. It was a happy crowd who sat around the long table in the dining room, though nine people did not even begin to fill the board. Alex sat in state at the head of his table, Aunt Tannie at the foot. Mrs. Wickfield was given the status of guest of honor at her host's right side, and Anne sat at his left. It was hardly a decorous feast, with Babe spilling her milk and several decrees having to be laid down as to what portion of wine should be allowed the twins and Loo on this special occasion. The twins would keep reverting to various barbaric deaths they planned to inflict on the Frenchies when they got to war, and even Robin came up with a few ingenious methods of torture.

"This is not an experience we will want to repeat," Alex said aside to Anne, but said it in such a condoning voice that she knew he didn't regret this one display of unformed manners.

He seemed more interested in looking contentedly down the table at his family than in eating. Any harshness she imagined in him before was not in evidence now. He shared his attention with Mrs. Wickfield as well, but it was to Anne that his eyes more often turned, till she formed the idea that her being beside him was at least some part of his pleasure.

"We'll have to throw a good big party now that I'm home," he said. "A ball, do you think, Anne, or a garden party? Or both? We'll have both. The children won't get much pleasure from a ball."

"Ah, a ball—we haven't had one since Charles died," Mrs. Tannie said. "That will be a deal of work for me, trying to shine us up enough to let the world in. You'd best be satisfied with a garden party."

Anne had no objection to either. Her mind flew to the white crepe resting on the shelf of Mumbleton's drapery shop. She would ask the price of it this very week and buy before it was gone. Alex put so many questions and statements to her that she assumed she was to be one of the prime movers in the preparations for his parties. When the meat was placed before Penholme for carving, he laughed nervously.

"This is the first time I've been called upon to act my role. Where do I start? I'm more nervous than on the eve of a battle. Imagine if we had guests present!"

Far from taking this as a slight, Anne was pleased that she and Mama were considered family. Their life was thin of company, and she worried that Alex's return might somehow change things. But till he married, at least, it

29

seemed she was to continue acting as an older sister. Whether it was ponies for the girls or new draperies for the blue room, Alex took for granted she would be not only interested but instrumental in the decision.

"Robin and I will join you shortly," he said when the meal was finished. "We plan to do the thing up right and claim the males' privilege of remaining behind for port. Rob has felt the lack of a man around the house, I think. I've promised him it will be part of our ritual now that I'm home."

It was with an air of importance that Robin drew Mrs. Wickfield's chair after dinner and stood back to watch the ladies and children leave the room. His chest was still swollen when he strolled into the saloon fifteen minutes later, but Anne found her attention rushing to Alex. He looked pale, and his step was slow. She noticed he held his right hand on his left shoulder, as though it bothered him.

He came directly to her. "We gulped it down as fast as we could," he said, and sat down.

"There was no hurry."

"Rob doesn't even care for wine. It was the idea of it that appealed to him. I prefer sherry myself now, not port. I like ritual—that's one thing I learned in Spain. It was the family rituals I missed—birthdays, Christmas, May Day." He was no longer rubbing his shoulder, but he sat stiffly, careful not to move it.

"Are you not feeling well, Alex? Surely your wound is not bothering you after all this time."

"Nothing to speak of. No proper medication was available on the boat, and it's become a little inflamed. I'll have my batman take a look at it before I retire."

"But is it not healed? I thought after such a long time it

30

must be only a scar. You should have Dr. Palmsey look at it."

"I'll call him tomorrow."

"It must have been a very bad wound! You told Aunt Tannie you were only grazed by the bullet."

"It was grazed rather deeply," he admitted. "I thought you would know by my tardy return that I'd become a Belem Ranger."

"What on earth is that?"

"A soldier who overstays his welcome at the Belem Convalescent Barracks. Malingerers, who are gun-shy."

His sudden wince was enough to tell her that Alex was not of that class. "Is it very painful?" she asked.

"I shouldn't have lifted Babe on my knee. I think I'd better have it looked at. I'll be right back."

"No, go to bed. You look pale as a sheet, Alex. We'll chat awhile to Aunt Tannie and leave early."

He looked alarmed. "No! Don't go. The children will be retiring right away. We haven't had a chance to talk. I want to give you and Auntie your presents."

"You can do it tomorrow."

"Please stay. I shan't be a moment," he said, and left before she had time to insist.

Robin crossed the room to take up his brother's place on the sofa. "Where's Alex off to?" he asked.

"His shoulder is bothering him."

"I told him he wasn't fit to ride this morning, but he said he'd be damned if a dragoon was going to arrive at Rosedale seated in a carriage like a lady. Simple vanity, you see. The curse of the Penholmes—present company always excepted," he added, smiling.

"It wasn't bothering him this morning."

"Maybe it was rearranging the master bedroom that did it. He wouldn't sleep in Charlie's bed last night, and was so eager to be rid of it this afternoon that he gave the footmen a hand dragging it out.''

''What?''

Robin, though he wouldn't harm a fly, had a thoughtless tongue. ''Uh-oh! Maybe I wasn't supposed to mention it. Alex didn't say not to. You must know there was no love lost between them, Annie.''

Her pity congealed to anger. ''I didn't know Alex had this unreasonable hatred of Charles. To refuse to sleep in his bed—it hardly sounds rational. My goodness, the man is dead. Why can't everyone forget that he wasn't perfect?''

''I daresay it will come, with time.''

Robin went on to discuss Sawburne, and across the room, Aunt Tannie poured a litany of complaints into Mrs. Wickfield's ears. ''He said he was ashamed to have the children seen in public in rags. 'So am I, sir!' says I. 'And ashamed to appear in Mumbleton's without paying something on the bill. You can't make jackets and shirts out of spiderwebs.' As to the house being dirty with a dozen maids sitting on their haunches drinking tea, people expect to be paid when they work.''

''It will be all right, Aunt Tannie. Alex is back now.''

He hadn't returned some fifteen minutes later when the children were sent off to bed. Anne went to the foot of the great staircase with them just as Alex came down. He was still pale but in less distress than before. He stopped to say good night to the children, and Anne turned to go back to the saloon.

''Wait!'' he said, and put his hand on her arm to detain her.

Physical touching was part and parcel of the exuberance of the Penholmes. They weren't the typical English

32

family who spurned physical contact after adolescence. It wasn't unusual for Robin or even the old earl to reach out and give one's arm a light blow during conversation. When they walked with a friend or family, it was as likely as not that an arm would be slung over the companion's shoulder, so this physical contact had no great significance, except that Alex had never done it before to Anne. His hand, laid on her arm unthinkingly, not only remained there but took a firmer grip on her. At last the children were gone, and he turned to her with still no sign of removing his hand.

"Did you get it looked after?" she asked. Her manner was cool, as she was annoyed at his refusing to sleep in Charles's bed. She made a point of disengaging herself from him.

"Lehman put a new bandage on it."

"Alex, surely it's not still bleeding!" she exclaimed, surprise overcoming annoyance. Her concern pleased him; she could see by the satisfaction in his eyes and the easing of the lines in his forehead.

"Only a little. It's my own vanity that is to blame— riding over to see you."

"Vanity? I think it more likely dragging a four-poster bed along the hall did the damage," she snipped.

His jaw tensed angrily. "I see you've been talking to my clapper-jawed brother." It was the worst possible moment to have to give a gift or accept one graciously, but the silver paper was in his hands. He held it out to her. "I have your present here. I hope you like it," he said stiffly.

The packet was so small she knew it must contain jewelry. She opened it, to reveal a chased silver ring with an opal at its center, surrounded by marquises. "It's beautiful! Thank you very much, Alex." The gift annoyed her in some way. It looked very expensive, for one thing; then, too, a ring had some suggestion of intimacy that struck her as unsuitable. "Did you steal it from a grandee?"

"It's not loot. I bought it for you. Don't you like it?" He took it from her, obviously intending to put it on her finger himself.

"I love it—but it looks very valuable."

"These things don't cost much in Spain. The merchants there aren't so grasping as ours have become." He held the ring for a moment, as if deciding which hand and which finger to place it on. Anne wore her grandmother's engagement ring on her right hand, and offered him her left. After a short pause, he slid it on to her third finger.

"Oh, not there! People will think it's an engagement ring!" she objected.

He gave a lighthearted laugh with a little sting of anger in it. "People *do* have a way of jumping to the wrong conclusion, don't they? Actually, it's too small for that finger. Your hands are larger than I remembered. It won't be mistaken for an engagement on your little finger, will it?"

"No, of course not." She splayed her fingers and looked at the ring. It was too large to suit her little finger. In fact, it could have gone over the knuckle of her third finger with a little push. It would look better on the third finger of her right hand. She experimented, Alex looking at her so closely that she felt self-conscious, and fumbled awkwardly. "There! I shall save it for very special occasions, like your ball," she said, smiling to ease the awkward moment. "It looks lovely, don't you think?"

"Very nice," he agreed. "I hope you have a lovelier one, one day, to wear on the other finger. I expect you have some parti in mind, as you objected so strenuously to

34

having that special digit encumbered with my metal. My family wrote so infrequently that I'm behind on the local gossip." His manner was casual, but his eyes, she thought, betrayed a concern for her answer.

"Oh, no. I am resigned to being maiden aunt to all my relatives' children," she answered in the same offhand manner.

He smiled, again casually. "We shall see. It's spring, the wooing season. Now I must give Aunt Alice her gift."

They returned to the saloon with his hand on her arm. Mrs. Wickfield's lips opened in a hopeful smile. "Mama is eager for her present, too," Anne said to conceal the true reason for that expression.

She was given an elegant brooch, of pearl surrounded by silver filigree. Its value was equal to that of Anne's ring, but the curiously staring eyes of all lingered questioningly on the ring.

"An opal, is it?" Mrs. Tannie asked. "They're bad luck, Alex. Didn't you know that? Annie doesn't need any more bad luck with the carriage wheel broken and Rosedale to be whisked out from under her as soon as her mother dies."

It was with a sigh of relief that they all heard her say her arthritis was killing her and she must go and lie down with a hot brick. Once she was gone, the remaining adults settled in for a long cose. They talked for two hours without a break and without any of them being aware of the time slipping by. Mrs. Wickfield was quick to smooth any waters that showed signs of roughening. At eleven, Robin and Alex accompanied the ladies home in the carriage.

"What a pleasant evening," Mrs. Wickfield said as they entered the house. "I haven't enjoyed myself so in an age. There's nothing like a family party, when you come down to it. What an interest Alex takes in those children. Almost as though he were their papa—in fact, a good deal more interest than the old earl ever took. As to Charles—I never saw any of the youngsters at the table when he was alive.''

''Alex missed them. I can't help wondering why he left, when he loves them so much.''

''I've often wondered myself. He never mentioned the army at all before he went away. He just walked over one day and said good-bye. Do you remember the day he came, Anne?''

''Yes, it was raining. He didn't stay a minute. I nearly fainted of shock.''

''I told him he was a ninny to go. Do you remember what he said?''

''No, what?''

''He said, 'I might as well.' I thought he'd give some rant about beating Boney or becoming a general or finding life dull here. But he said, 'I might as well,' so half-heart-edly. I can't imagine what made him do it.''

''We've never known Alex at all. That's what it comes down to.''

From the pensive expression in her daughter's eyes, Mrs. Wickfield was encouraged to believe mystery was no impediment to love. ''We know he's Lord Penholme—no question of that,'' she pointed out helpfully. ''A pity he hadn't slid that ring on a different finger, eh?''

''I don't feel the ring was a suitable gift. I wish he had given me the brooch.''

''Maybe it's a hint of things to come. I take it as a good omen.''

''Or a bad one. Opals are bad luck.''

''Good gracious, you mustn't listen to that doomsayer.

It would be the greatest luck in the world if you could marry Alex."

Anne stared into the opal, watching the flash of red and orange and yellow, which turned to green and blue as she twisted the ring on her finger. Yes, it would be suitable in every way for her to marry Alex, an excellent parti, except that she didn't love him. She loved Charles.

Chapter Four

Mrs. Wickfield was in high spirits after the dinner. She had detected a burgeoning interest in her daughter by Lord Penholme and fully expected to see him at their door soon and often. His absence on the first day, she excused on the grounds of his bad shoulder acting up. The second day it rained rather hard. "With that wound, he is wise to remain home," she said, but in a voice indicating that in affairs of the heart, discretion was not the better part of wisdom.

"He never paid us much attention, Mama. Why would he come here again so soon?" Anne asked blandly. Yet she felt a rankling at his continued absence. Every time she looked at her ring she thought of him, and of his consciously trying to put it on her left hand. That question about her having a suitor in mind was quite pointed as well. If a man was interested enough to drop a few hints, one expected him to follow it up. But really, she was half relieved.

Lord Robin was on much closer terms with the family, and on the third day, late in the afternoon, he dropped in for a cup of tea. "Good gracious, you look like a scarecrow!" Anne exclaimed when she beheld the muddy spectacle in the saloon. "What on earth have you been doing?"

"I've been at the tenant farms with Alex."

"His wound is progressing satisfactorily after moving Charles's bed, is it?" Anne asked.

"He hasn't mentioned it, nor did he bother calling Palsmey. From the way he's been digging ditches and hauling rocks and whatnot, I assume it's better."

"What is the purpose of all this labor?" Mrs. Wickfield inquired.

Robin shook his head in bewilderment. "I think he's *loco na cabeza,*" he said. "That's Spanish. I'm learning a few words from him. He turned Buckram off, you see. That's the fellow Charles hired after Alex left. He's turned out to be a regular *bandido.* I daresay it's my fault for not having kept a closer eye on things, but truth to tell, I hadn't a notion about farming. Buckram said he'd had the fields marled, and the bonehead tenants never told me otherwise. Alex says he'd be surprised if there's a teaspoon of lime in an acre. He sent Buckram to the rightabout—dismissed him, and without giving him a character."

"That seems rather hard!" Anne exclaimed.

"That's the way Alex means to run things in future. Including me."

"You are not a thing, Robin."

"Ain't I? I'm beginning to feel like one. A dashed tired thing. *People* don't get up at six in the morning, do they? Of course, he sends me to bed as soon as ever the sun sets, so I'm awake early."

"Why is he doing this?"

"Oh, he plans to make a man of me."

"Obviously not a *gentleman,*" Anne said, running her eyes over his mud-splattered jacket and buckskins. His

39

boots were so muddied they had been removed at the door.

The tea arrived, and Robin leaned against the sofa with a weary sigh. "Do you know what we did this afternoon?" he asked in a voice that defied them to let their imagination soar.

"Took mud baths?" Mrs. Wickfield inquired, for she feared his elbows might be dirtying the sofa.

"You're not far out. We dug ditches like a couple of common peons. Looking for tiles, which Buckram said he put in, but the bogs after that rain must have told a mawworm there were no tiles there. And, of course, there weren't, so Alex lined up the tenants with shovels to dig a ditch. The worse of the flood must be channeled away or the crops will drown. At least I think that's why we did it," he added uncertainly.

Mrs. Wickfield came to indignant attention. "You never mean Lord Penholme spent his afternoon digging a ditch!"

"We supervised," Robin explained. "The way Alex supervises things is by digging in and working harder than anyone. He was just waiting for me to knuckle under, so, of course, I had to keep the pace. He says an officer's job is to lead his men, not to bring up the rear."

"Why does he not buy tiles and have the job done properly?" Anne asked.

"*Quién sabe?* More Spanish. I expect he's either too poor or too clutch-fisted. He's been ripping up at Aunt Tannie, too, till she's threatening to walk out on us. She does wear a body's nerves to a razor edge after a while, but all the poor woman did is ask for money to buy linen. With dozens of girls sitting on their hands all day long, he didn't see why they couldn't get busy and mend the sheets and things, instead of buying new ones. Lord, they're so thin you could spit through the best linen in the house. Oh, I'll tell you, ladies, he's come home a changed man. He was always a bit sour, but he's turned *mean.*''

"Well, Mama," Anne said, "you were regretting he had not come to call. We must count ourselves fortunate to have been spared."

The tea had a softening effect on Robin. "I didn't mean to make him out a monster," he said. "I daresay once he gets things set to rights, we'll have smoother sailing. The estate is certainly a shambles, and he didn't cut up so stiff with me for not having done a better job of overseeing Buckram. He apologized to Aunt Tannie, too, once he had settled down. She has no cleverness, poor woman. She hit him up for the money the minute he got home from the bank, when anyone could see by his scowl his pockets are to let. It's been a bit of a tough homecoming for him."

"He's making it tougher on himself," Mrs. Wickfield said. "He can't expect to undo all Buckram's harm in a week. He should go at it more slowly, relax a little. Spend some time getting reacquainted with the neighbors," she added meaningfully.

"He does seem to get some pleasure from being with the children," Robin said. "He never rips up at them, and during our *siesta,* he tells me a lot of interesting things about Spain. We're in shallow waters, and it is for the men of the family—he means me and him—to paddle us out. It gives a fellow a good feeling, but I must let off steam somewhere, you know, and if I do it with Willie and Bung, they'll go running back to Alex, for they think he's all the crack. *Número uno.*''

Robin's frown had eased to a rather fond smile as he changed his tune, and Mrs. Wickfield's expression changed along with it. "I expect Alex has some long-term plans for your future, Robin—something more than digging ditches.''

"Oh, certainly he has. We talk about it all the time. As he is so keen on teaching me how to run an estate, I have some hopes of getting our smaller farm, Sawburne, pretty soon.''

The conversation turned to local gossip, and in half an hour, Robin rose to take his leave. ''I don't know when I can sneak away to visit you again. Tonight Alex is having the tenants to the Hall for a planning rally, to see if they can share teams and plows and whatnot and work more efficiently. Oh, and to arrange a cottage for Nudgely's son, who is marrying another tenant's daughter—the bracket-faced Stinson girl. They can't afford to build, so he has to sweet-talk Mrs. Nudgely into leaving the family cottage and move in with a sister in the village, for the Stinson chit won't live with her mother-in-law. If he can't nudge the old lady to town, he's afraid we'll have Mrs. Nudgely cluttering up the Hall.''

Mrs. Wickfield nodded in approval. ''He was always a good manager.''

"Yes, he says the cottages have to produce, and a widow, especially Mrs. Nudgely, ain't producing anything but trouble. She was always a spiteful harpy. She don't even keep a cow—her neighbors say she turned the milk sour at a glance.''

Robin put on his boots and left. *''Adiós*, ladies.'' He was whistling as he strode to the door. His shoulders were held at a straighter angle, his head a little higher, his pace brisker, as of a man with things to do. Yes, he looked more like a man than a boy. Already the change was noticeable.

It rained again on Sunday, and with only a gig at their disposal, the Wickfield ladies said their prayers at home.

The weather prevented callers, and by Monday, Anne felt she had to get out of the house or she would scream. She harnessed up Mrs. Dobbin for a ramble through the meadows. No faster pace or longer trip was possible on the jaded nag. The meadow was spangled with wild flowers. Pied daisies and silver-white lady's-smocks, blue violets, and buttercups tempted her from the saddle to garner a bouquet. She trod carefully, lifting her skirt to protect it from the damp grass.

The sun beat warmly on her shoulders from the azure-blue arc overhead, with soft cottonwool puffs of clouds floating high. Despite the beautiful serenity, Anne felt some vague dissatisfaction with life—some sense of urgency, of time slipping by and nothing changing. Things should change in spring; something new and wonderful and exciting should happen. She had looked forward to Penholme's arrival as possibly bringing an increase in social activity, but no parties had been thrown. There had been no more talk of the ball or garden party. Alex was too busy digging ditches. If it were Charles who was home, how different things would have been. She had felt on the day of Alex's arrival that he had changed, but he had only become more pronounced in his usual working routine. He even kept Robin from calling as much as he used to.

She was bent low, gathering her flowers. Penholme didn't see her, but he saw Mrs. Dobbin tethered to a post and stopped to look around. When he spotted Anne, he dismounted and advanced on foot. He was within a few yards before she heard him. Her instinctive response upon seeing him was annoyance: whether because he had come or because he had not come for so long, she didn't know. Perhaps it was only that he was not his elder brother.

"Buenas tardes, señorita," he said, and removed his hat, making a playful bow.

She again had that sensation of being with a stranger. Robin occasionally spoke Spanish, too, but coming from him, it was only amusing. On Alex's lips, the words sounded softer, more intimate—romantic. It was the tone of voice that accounted for it. Yet as she looked at him, she found nothing romantic in his appearance. He wore an old and ill-fitting jacket. Mud had hardened to gray blobs on his top boots and buckskins.

"Hello, Alex," she said, and continued picking her flowers, for she had come across a full patch of daisies.

"I have been meaning to call at Rosedale."

She gave a casual shrug. "I'm sure you're very busy."

Alex reached down his hand to pull her up. "You have enough flowers. This is my meadow." He smiled. "I don't mind a little looting, but leave some for the bees."

"I made sure a horn-and-hoof farmer like you would approve of garnering all of nature's bounty."

"So I do. Honey is the bounty these blossoms provide."

"But you don't have any hives."

"I shall soon. I have already suggested it to a few of my tenant wives who are past the cares of child-rearing."

He took her arm and began walking back to the horses. "Poor old Mrs. Dobbin," he said, shaking his head at the sway-backed jade, who chomped the grass desultorily.

"Poor Annie," she added. "I used to be a fair-to-middling horsewoman. The only skill Mrs. Dobbin requires is patience."

"There are plenty of mounts at the Hall. Why don't you borrow one?"

"You don't know your Shakespeare, Alex. 'Neither a borrower nor a lender be.' If you don't mean to *give* me one, then I shall just hobble along on Mrs. Dobbin till

44

she cocks up her toes and dies." She spoke in jest, and as Alex smiled, she felt no fear he had misread it into a hint.

"I shan't detain you. I know you keep yourself very busy," she said, and began to untie the rein.

"No, really! I'm not such a slave to duty that I can't spend a social moment with my favorite neighbor."

"If you have time to spare, might I suggest a change of clothes—or at least that you have your valet take a good stiff brush to your jacket and boots? We are not accustomed to seeing the lord of Penholme in soiled boots."

"A little dirt never hurt anyone," he said, but with a conscious look as he examined his soiled outfit. "The fields are wet as bedamned."

"Oh, really, Alex," she scolded him. "Couldn't you have your workmen do that rough labor? Robin has been compl—telling us how you go on."

"Complaining?" he asked swiftly.

"Telling us."

"I've been firm with him. It's not good for a young man to have nothing to do. He ends up falling into mischief."

Anne read an indirect slur against Charles into his comment and felt a hot rush of anger. "You need not worry that he'll follow in his other brother's footsteps, if that is your meaning."

Alex didn't deny it. "There's good stuff in him—a fine lad, but lying in bed till ten in the morning and spending his evenings in the taverns isn't the way to develop him. He must learn to pull his weight. There's no free ride."

She shook her head. "All work and duty. You haven't changed a bit, Alex. Why don't you relax and enjoy yourself? Only look how beautiful the day is."

He scarcely glanced at the meadow before his eyes settled on her face. "I'll let you do the relaxing. I can't relax

45

with my estate crumbling into decay around me. And I can't afford a good steward at the moment. Soon I hope to be less busy. I've been looking forward to this spring for a long time." He gazed at the meadow, then up at the cloud-billowed sky, and last, he turned his eyes to the gray walls of Penholme, which soared into the heavens. His face wore a peculiar expression, compounded of nostalgia, impatience, frustration, and determination. "A long time," he repeated softly.

She felt attuned to this mellower mood. "You always loved Penholme. It must have been awful, being away from home," she said gently.

He turned and smiled at her. It was the stranger whose brown eyes examined her. She knew before he said a word that he would speak in that new tongue she could not understand but that somehow beguiled her. *"Tiene razón, más estoy mejor, querida."*

"How romantic that sounds. I suppose it only means you must leave to ring a peal over someone at the Hall for wasting time or candles or food."

"I see Robin has painted me in vivid colors—a deep-dyed villain. I can't think when he found time to visit you."

"He wasted only a moment in such dissipation, I promise you. And the picture wasn't totally black. He was quite flattered that you called him a man. Mama feels you are trimming him into line very well."

The smile that lit his eyes was no longer nostalgic. There was a spark of mischief in it. "I didn't foresee any difficulty in bringing Aunt Alice around my thumb. It is her recalcitrant *hija* whose disapproval troubles me—very much."

"I wish you would speak English," she scowled, but

really it was more a pout than a scowl. Something in him brought out this flirtatious side of her nature.

"You scourged me with Shakespeare. Let me reciprocate the offense by giving you Dr. Johnson. A man with a second language is like a lady with a new petticoat; he is not contented till he has showed it off. I am only doing what I must, you know, by keeping my nose to the grindstone. Soon I shall be free to join Robin in the dissipation of taking tea with you, if you will permit me."

"I should be flattered. We were never accustomed to many calls from you. Does this mean you are turning over a new leaf, becoming sociable?" she asked archly. She hoped this would lead to setting the date for his ball.

"It ill becomes the lord of the Hall to be a surly hermit. May I come tomorrow?"

"Anytime. We are usually home and never bar our door to callers from the Hall."

"That dilutes my victory, Anne," he teased her. "I shall leave before you ask me to bring Aunt Tannie and the children along."

There was no mounting block, and though Anne was perfectly capable of mounting Mrs. Dobbin by herself, she assumed Alex would offer her a hand.

It wasn't till then that she noticed he held his left arm at an awkward angle. "Alex, are you all right?" she asked.

"I'm fine," he said at once, and tried to assist her, but it was obvious the effort caused him pain.

"I trust you haven't been moving furniture again," she said with a sapient look.

"No, mud, which is a deal heavier. As Robin saw fit to tell you I moved Charles's bed, he should have told the reason. It was the mattress I objected to, Anne, not the former occupant. I would have liked to sleep in the bed of my father and grandfather. Since I was wounded, however, I have to sleep on a very firm bed. The springs in that old four-poster are a hundred years old. Truth to tell, I'm no longer comfortable smothered in dusty bed canopies either. I like to feel the air move around me. It lets me know I'm alive."

"That wasn't the impression I got from Robin."

"It is not the one I gave. I don't like being an invalid. Everyone's concern for my shoulder is already a nuisance to them. Must I burden them with my bad back and my nightmares—?" He stopped and gave her an impatient frown.

The pain was visible on his face, pinching around the eyes and mouth. What horrors had he been through, that had left him so ravaged? "Oh, Alex, I'm sorry," she said impulsively, and reached for his hands. He clutched at her fingers, holding them in a painful grip. She could feel the metal from her ring pressing her other fingers. She noticed Alex was looking at it.

"What grand occasion were you anticipating, all alone in the meadow?" he asked.

"Grand occasions are few and far between. If I am to wear my ring at all, I must wear it just anywhere—to the meadow, the village. . . ."

When he lifted his eyes, they stood still a moment, just looking at each other. There was some scalding tension in the air, some feeling so intense it startled her.

"You—you had best get home," she said breathlessly.

"Yes, but tomorrow I'll call on you, as I promised."

"All right."

She watched as he awkwardly mounted his bay, using only one hand, and rode away. She was still there five minutes later, staring after him, with a little smile lifting her lips. As she stood thinking, the smile vanished. She shouldn't have been so hard on Alex—cutting up at him for having muddy boots, when he was only doing what he had to do. It was none of her concern if he didn't want to sleep in Charles's bed, for that matter. But he behaved as though it *were* her concern. He looked as if . . . How foolish of her. It was spring—that was the trouble.

Such a beautiful, sunny spring day. She buried her face in the flowers and gave a little laugh of pure joy.

Chapter Five

In anticipation of Alex's call the next morning, Anne had her hair teased into a basket of curls in a fashion not usually attempted but for a party. She felt strangely disappointed when he had still not arrived by midafternoon. It began to look as though he had truly reverted to his old way of neglecting them. She thought she must have read too much into that interlude in the meadow. It was just the beauty of the spring day that lent the incident that special air. At four, Robin cantered up and lounged into their saloon to make his brother's apologies.

"Congratulations. I see you've slipped the leash," Anne said.

"I've been let off. Alex is sick as a dog."

"What is the matter?" Mrs. Wickfield demanded.

"He called Palmsey to have a go at his wound. He's pretty well knocked up after the sawbones's visit," he explained.

"How is his wound?" Anne asked eagerly.

Robin shivered. "Ugly! His shoulder looks like a raw beefsteak. I had no idea it was still open. It became infected again on the boat, but it couldn't have been very well healed to have broken out like this. Palmsey cauterized it. I very nearly passed out, for he made me hold Alex down. You could smell the burning flesh; I even heard it sizzle. I shan't tackle a rare steak for a few days, I can tell you.''

"Oh!'' Anne's hand flew to her lips, and she turned pale. "How is he?''

"He passed out, thank Dios. Palmsey got a cup of brandy into him before he branded him. He came around again after lunch, but he won't be up for a day or two. Imagine his not telling us how bad it is. But Alex was always one to keep things to himself. We should have known when it took him so long to come home. He would have come running as soon as he could.''

"Good gracious, what has Palmsey to say about it?'' Mrs. Wickfield asked. "Is he going to be all right?''

"Certainly. Palmsey will bring him around. Alex is merry as a grig. His big fear was that he'd loose the arm—they wanted to chop it off at Belem, you know. There's no chance of that now. With good food and clean bandages, he'll pull around. He's pretty disgusted with the thing—Alex, I mean, not Palmsey. I daresay having a *real* wound is a pleasant change from doling out headache powders for Palmsey.''

"It'll slow Alex down,'' Mrs. Wickfield said, worried.

"Devil a bit of it. He's got his man of business coming to see him tomorrow. He'll interview him from his bed. He don't intend to waste a minute. No, it's the looks of the wound that disgust him.''

"No one will see it,'' Anne pointed out. "He should be happy it's not his face that's disfigured.''

"His wife will see it,'' Robin answered. " 'How do you offer a charred and mangled old carcass like this to anyone?' he asked me. Palmsey admits there'll be a scar.''

51

Mrs. Wickfield lifted a curious brow. "Talking of getting married, is he?"

"He will be, now that he's head of the house," Robin allowed with an arch little smile toward Anne, who pretended not to see it.

A Penholme would not be expected to leave without taking tea—Lord Robin in particular was a veritable sponge—so the visit lasted half an hour. The subject moved on to some repining that the visit to Sawburne must be delayed awhile. No call was expected from the gentlemen on the morrow. Mrs. Wickfield mentioned riding over to Penholme in the gig the next morning, but Anne declined such hard chasing as to go after a man who was sick in bed. Aunt Tannie brought the girls to call in the afternoon, so some news was heard. Alex was recuperating from his treatment, and seeing to business, as Robin had said.

"Might discouraged, he is, I can tell you," Mrs. Tannie informed them. She was puffing from the exertion of getting her stout frame up the stairs and into a chair. Mrs. Tannie dressed quite independently of fashion, in a boisterously flowered gown of red and white that played awful havoc with her rosy complexion.

"Things are bad, are they?" Mrs. Wickfield asked.

"Wretched. Now that he's home, you know, the tradesmen in the village are sending in their bills. My, such a lot of them. I'm sure we had a dozen there this morning alone. The cobbler—well, boots for the lot of them all these years, and the twins growing so fast they must be shod twice a year. A bill for three hundred from him."

"Surely not so much!" Mrs. Wickfield gasped. More than half her annual income seemed a high price for boots.

"There were still some of Charlie's top boots unpaid. He ordered a pair with white rims and never did wear them either. His Beau Brummell boots, he called them. Charlie was such a stylish dresser," she added fondly. "Then there were the miller, the draper, the general store—you might as well say we had the village to call, and poor Alex so fagged he should have stayed in bed."

"You never mean he went down to see them!" Anne exclaimed.

"He's bound and bent to pretend he's getting better. That lad will never be whole again. What wasn't shot away in Spain was burned away by Palmsey. And you'll never guess what, Alice," Aunt Tannie continued, hardly stopping to draw air. "The dovecot that holds nothing but swallows—Charles never paid for that. He had it built the year he came into his own. Imagine, five years it's been sitting in the yard, and us never knowing it wasn't paid for. The same with the addition he had put on to the stables. I hadn't the heart to tell Alex, but I was never paid a penny either, and Charles *did* say I'd get a hundred pounds a year, not that I need it, for I can always charge everything, of course. Still, he said I'd get it. Not that I really expected I would," she added matter-of-factly.

"Of course he'll pay you," Anne said, but the complete pessimist knew better. She gave Anne a sorry, disillusioned look and launched forth on another sea of complaints.

After Dr. Palmsey had dropped in for a chat on his way to the Hall to check on his patient, he said ever so politely to Mrs. Tannie on his way out that he wouldn't bother sending his bill for a bit, till his lordship was feeling stouter. He mentioned the girls' measles, Robin's sprained ankle, and Mrs. Tannie's own rheumatism—all services rendered without payment. Though he reaffirmed there was no hurry, it was clear that he expected his money soon.

"I begin to think we'll all land in the poorhouse," Aunt Tannie declared, and had to revive herself with a good strong cup of tea and two scones before she could continue her litany. "According to Robin, the rents ain't coming the way they should be, either."

A pile of tradesmen's bills was an unpleasant welcome but could hardly be more than an embarrassment to the lord of Penholme. Not even Anne felt any real disquiet.

On the third day, Alex was sufficiently recovered to leave the house but was not well enough to ride his mount. He came to Rosedale in his late brother's curricle, with his batman, Lehman, at the reins. As well as a spanking team of grays to pull the sporting carriage, there was a handsome bay mare being led behind it. This was tethered to the mulberry tree in the front yard, and Anne was invited out to see it as soon as Alex had made his bows to the ladies.

During the time of his recovery, she had decided she must be a little kinder to Alex, at least till she came to know him better. He couldn't help not being Charles; it was unfair to judge him against a paragon. She would get to know him for himself. "Oh, you've brought Lady to visit," she said, wondering why he should have done so, as she was not saddled, and the fact of his arm being in a sling made it unlikely he meant to ride.

"I've brought her to stay, if you'll have her."

"To stay? Alex—this is not a gift! I can't accept her. It's too much. Oh, you thought I was hinting!"

"She's of no use to us. Not frisky enough for Rob or me, and too much for Loo to handle."

"Sell her, then. She'll fetch a good price. From what Aunt Tannie tells us, you can use the money."

"You must cut everything she says in half. You would think she were Mrs. Job, the way she wails and moans. I've already sorted out the cattle and sent off to auction what we don't need. Robin and the groom have taken them over to Eastleigh today. We've cut down from two dozen nags to ten. They're to pick up a pair of ponies for the girls. Lady's a beauty, Anne. Don't you like her?''

''She's adorable, but I can't accept such a gift,'' she said calmly but firmly.

Alex made a dismissing wave with his free hand. ''She wouldn't bring what she's worth at auction, and after giving the barn its commission, what would be left? I want you to have her. Very likely Charlie bought her with you in mind.'' His bright eyes held a question as he looked steadily at her.

''She wasn't bought for me. He had her for a year and never mentioned such a thing.''

''I don't know what else he had in mind, buying a lady's mount,'' he said reasonably.

''He had a great many ladies visiting. No doubt he got her to have a spare there in case any of his guests wished to ride.''

''She's too fine an animal to use as a spare, for just anyone to ride.''

''Charlie liked the best,'' she reminded him.

''That's why I thought she must be for you,'' he answered in a rallying way that might have been a joke, though there was enough admiration in his regard to cause some doubt. ''Quite sure she wasn't?''

Anne felt a flush brighten her cheeks. ''Positive. Charles never offered me Lady or anything else. Any other mount, I mean.''

Alex looked at her for a long moment before saying, ''I see.'' She had the feeling there was more being discussed than a mount, and his next question confirmed it. ''Never offered you his name either, Anne? I'm sure it was his intention to do so. Did you refuse him?''

It was hard to read his expression. It was intent, and he was keenly interested in her reply, but what else was in it she could only guess. "He didn't offer the name or the mount. I've already told you I should have refused the latter."

"And the former? The name?"

Anne would no more have refused an offer from Charles than she would have cut off her arm, but she felt a sudden disinclination to say so. Just why she hesitated to confirm what was a pretty well known suspicion was unclear to her. Perhaps it was no more than pride. "We ladies like to keep our secrets," she said with a little toss of her shoulders. The motion held a touch of flirtation.

It emboldened Alex to adopt a similar tone. He inclined his head to her and said, "I think you would have made a charming Lady Penholme."

"I see what it is. Dissatisfied with a mere three sisters, you wanted another."

"No, I didn't want that at all, I promise you." His smile faded as he stood gazing at her. When he spoke again, he was deadly serious. "Did you love him?" he asked simply.

With equal directness, she said, "Yes, very much. All the girls were fascinated with Charles. Oh, I know his reputation smacked of every sin in the Bible, but rakehells are attractive to women, you know."

"They make fine daydreams, but less fine husbands, I daresay."

"It was just a daydream, so there's no point discussing it further."

Alex nodded silently. The ensuing pause was long and uncomfortable. Unable to sustain the tension, Anne sought to lighten the mood. "I love Lady, too, but I could not accept her from either Lord Penholme."

He hunched his shoulders. "She's no good to me. I held her back from auction for you. It's more bother than it's worth to take one mount over to Eastleigh another time. Come now, accept her. You'll hurt her feelings. She'll only be eating her head off in my stable, with no one to exercise her. See how frisky she is—dying to be ridden."

It was a sore temptation, the more so as there was really nothing wrong in accepting a gift from the Hall. There were precedents aplenty—in fact, Mrs. Dobbin had been a gift from the old earl. But somehow Anne was not happy to accept one from Alex.

"You can't possibly be getting a decent ride on your old Dobbin," he persisted. "Lady likes you—see how she's nuzzling your shoulder."

"So would she be nuzzling you if you massaged her neck on this side," Anne said, laughing. "But we are retrenching. When Mrs. Dobbin cocks up her toes, we shall be glad. Her formidable appetite is eating us out of house and home."

"So are we retrenching at the Hall. A new regime has set it, if you don't know it already from all my complaining relatives. You must have heard of the affair of the thread-bare linen. I'm only trying to get you to take on the feed of this glutton," he said.

"You did not use to be so stubborn, Alex. I see your trick. Next you will send those ravenous twins down to batten themselves on us. Thank you, but I really cannot accept your gift."

Far from pokering up at the charge of stubbornness, he appeared pleased with it. "I shan't sell her. May I leave her here for you to use till Loo grows into her?"

She tossed up her hands in surrender. "Very well, I'll say yes, before you're put to some other lying shift to force her on me, since it's clear you mean to have your way."

"You see how quickly the title has gone to my head. I expect folks to cater to my every whim. Next thing you know, I'll be expecting you to jump to your feet when I enter the room."

"I should be happy to do it if this is the way you pay your toadeaters. She's a beauty, Alex. Thank you for being so imaginative in your insistence." As she patted Lady's muzzle, the sun caught the marquises in her ring, reminding her of that other gift.

"Should you be out in the sun so long, Alex? Would you like to go inside?"

"I'm fine. Let's walk a little," he suggested. "It's such a fine day."

They left Lady behind and strolled around to the garden, back through the orchard. Again Alex put his hand on Anne's elbow, not moving it till they came to a stone bench and sat down. He gazed into the sun-dappled roof of leaves with a wistful smile.

"I missed three seasons of blossoms. Three springs—the finest time of the year. I love to see the petals blowing in the air, like snowflakes. It's strange, the things you miss when you're away from home. You can't think how often I imagined it, when I was slogging through swamps, being eaten alive by flies and lice, or trekking over some rough mountain with the sun burning my eyes. It hasn't changed. That's the miracle. It's still so green and cool and fresh, just as I remembered it. Next year the petals will form again, and fall."

She studied his rugged profile, which gazed unblinking at the trees. His rapture imbued them with some special charm. Three years—three of his best years, and hers. "Why did you go Alex?" she asked softly. "It was very sudden, wasn't it?"

"No, I was five years working up to it, actually."

Charles had been earl for five years when Alex had left. That was the impetus, then.

"You never said anything about it."

"I'm the oyster of the family. We need one, you know, when the rest of us cackle like geese."

"I wouldn't call you an oyster."

"Wouldn't you, Duck?" he asked, turning to smile at her. It was a warm, intimate smile that eased the harshness of his expression. "We used to call you Duck when you were two years old and waddling like one."

"What a memory! You must have been only a child yourself."

"The name lingered a long while. You were called Duck till you were twelve—and I a callow seventeen."

"I seem to remember," she said vaguely, but what she remembered more clearly was that Charles used to call her Duck occasionally, right up to the time he died. The dark eyes smiling intimately into hers looked suddenly very like Charles's eyes. How odd! She'd never noticed that resemblance between the brothers before.

"Do you remember the day you forbade it?" he asked.

"No."

"I do. It was the Easter Charles came down from Oxford and gave you the white kitten that was supposed to be for Bung. He bawled all night long. You must remember the kitten. I was so gauche as to call you Duck in front of Charles, when you had taken into your head to flirt with him. Your first effort at batting your lashes—inexpertly done, but a pretty performance. I daresay the inopportune moment I chose to call you Duck accounted for your rant."

"I called him Whitey—the kitten."

"And you called me—no, some things are best forgotten."

"I had forgotten all about the incident," she said, dismissing it as of little interest. "Alex, why did you leave? Now that you've turned voluble, perhaps I can pry it out of you."

"Not yet," he said. "Later."

"You're just giving yourself airs, to be mysterious and interesting."

"You don't have to put on airs to be interesting. You're interesting, and you're the most airless girl I know."

"I sound remarkably stuffy—absolutely airless."

"Never! Airless, but not stuffy. A rare combination."

"I sound like a vacuum. Absence has made your heart grow fonder of more than trees and petals. If I hear you praise the sermon on Sunday, I shall know it's homesickness speaking, for you always abhorred Danfer's sermons, and they have not improved during your absence. In fact, they haven't changed."

"Then I shall be sure to disparage it, for I don't want you to take the notion my praise was insincere. Notice I don't call it flattery, Duck?"

"Since you're determined to be gallant, I shan't discourage you, but let me slip you a clue, Mr. Oyster. Your future gallantry is not to take the form of expensive gifts."

"Oh, expensive!" he scoffed. "I don't know what Rob was thinking of not to have given you Lady years ago. You should have suggested it, Anne."

"Of course I should. I really ought to have hit him up for a new team and carriage while I was about it. The kitchen roof is not all it should be either. I wonder he didn't get it fixed for us before now. Really, he's been very behindhand in looking after Mama and me."

"I've passed the margin from gallantry to gaucherie, have I? You make it easy on my pinched purse, forcing me to limit my gallantry to mere words."

They returned to the house, but on this occasion Alex did no more than say good day to Mrs. Wickfield before leaving to go into the village. "I must find out how much I am in hawk to all the merchants," he said. "Some of them came to the Hall, which fills me with terror. I should have thought they'd wait till I went to them. Such an undue eagerness for my company makes me fear the sum is staggering. I hope there is enough money left from the auction to begin tiling."

"Tannie told us three hundred pounds for the cobbler," Mrs. Wickfield mentioned.

"I should realize between one and two thousand from what Rob took to the auction. Closer to two—I sold off a few carriages we didn't need, as well. A sky-blue phaeton and a rattan curricle seemed an unnecessary extravagance. Even Rob won't drive in them."

After he left, Mrs. Wickfield cast a few animadversions on the late earl's extravagance. "What a rotten kettle of fish for Alex to come home to," she griped.

But as he spoke of picking up a couple of thousand from selling his excess stable, no one could worry about his solvency. Anne's mother did not find the loan of Lady exorbitant and smiled softly to herself. She suspected the offer of his hand might follow before too long.

"Did he say anything interesting while you were walking?" she asked hopefully.

"We were just talking about the old days."

"It might be best not to harp on the past, Annie," Mrs. Wickfield advised. "A young gentleman wouldn't like to hear about his lady's other flirts."

"Good heavens, Mama, we weren't talking about Charles," Anne said. "Just a mention in passing . . ."

But really they had talked about Charles quite a lot. Specifically about her and Charles, and she had been too naive to disclaim her interest. What was the point? She *had* loved Charles—one couldn't erase the past. But somehow she rather wished she had softened it a little.

Chapter Six

Anne was surprised to discover her muscles were stiff the next morning from her short ride on Lady. The best cure was to do exactly what she wanted; namely, remount and go for a longer ride. As the backhouse boy was busy cleaning ashes from stove and fireplace, she was confined to the private land between Penholme and Rosedale, but this left her plenty of choice. How exhilarating it was to be flying through meadows with the wind in her face and a smooth pacer under her, to be able to jump a stream instead of urging Mrs. Dobbin through it. When a low fence suddenly appeared in front of her, she summoned her courage and put Lady over it. There! She hadn't done that in five years. She had forgotten the soaring joy of a real ride. When she became warm from her exertions, she drove through the shaded spinney at a slower pace, to admire the wild flowers and the soft gurgle of a brook. The morning was perfect—nearly. A companion to ride with would have completed the pleasure.

From there she rode around the edge of the sheep field to admire the gamboling new lambs, which looked like little clouds fallen from the sky. After an hour's hard riding she was tired, but the day was too fine to go home.

In the distance the stone walls of Penholme rose. As she approached it from the rear, the first person she saw was Alex. He already had his arm out of the sling. He was talking to some workmen. When he saw her, he waved and walked forward to meet her, leaving the men behind.

"Now aren't you glad you came down off your high ropes and took Lady?" he asked. "You make a beautiful pair."

"More gallantry! Lady and I thank you. I didn't come to take you from your work, Alex. I'll go in to say hello to Aunt Tannie."

"I'll join you presently. Wait till I come."

"Yes, milord." She gave him a pert smile.

"That was a request, however incivilly worded."

"It had the air of a military command."

"No, no. I've sold out. It's my new title that makes me so arrogant, Duck." He laughed and turned back to the workmen.

Loo and Babe were in the stable, admiring the ponies Robin had chosen for them at Eastleigh. The stable looked half empty. Anne mentally tallied up what mounts had been put on the block. He'd kept the grays for the curricle, the bays for the family carriage, a hack and hunter each for himself and Rob, a hack each for the twins, and he'd bought the ponies for the girls. Just what a man in his position would consider essential.

While she was complimenting the girls on their Welsh ponies, Alex joined them. "Here, up you go," he said to Babe.

"Alex, your arm!" Anne cautioned.

"I can lift Babe with one arm," he said, and did so, hoisting her up on the pony's back. Like all the Penholmes, she had a natural affinity for horses. She was soon jogging around the yard as easily as she walked. Loo had scrambled up on her pony by herself and went after her.

"Imagine Babe not being mounted till she's six," Alex said ruefully.

"She's still a baby."

"A Penholme baby! Rosalie was hunting when she was eight. And look at Loo—what an awkward set of hands. Here, Loo!" He went after her and rearranged the reins between her fingers, urging her to sit straight and not pull on the line.

This done, he stood back to watch. "They should be in the schoolroom today, but I had to let them try out their ponies. As far as that goes, that governess. . . . Where did she come from, anyway?"

"Sussex, I believe."

"Literalist! I meant what is her background. I stepped into her schoolroom yesterday and heard a few paragraphs of a gothic novel. She's not at all well spoken. I don't relish telling her she must leave, but the girls need a better teacher than that."

"I don't know what her background is, but she is engaged to the local schoolteacher. Perhaps if you intrude yourself into the schoolroom with gentle hints of geography and grammar, she'll see fit to marry him in a hurry."

"How long has she been here?"

"Since shortly after you left."

"That's what I thought," he said. His manner of saying it told her what was in his mind. Charles's work, hiring an unsuitable employee because she was young and pretty.

A groom, and there was an excess of them with the diminished stable, was called to oversee the girls' lesson, and Anne and Alex entered the house.

They met Mrs. Tannie just coming from conference with cook. She ordered tea and went with them to the gold saloon. "How much do you owe the builder?" she asked bluntly.

"Fifty for the dovecot, two hundred and fifty for the stables. That was Coulter, the builder, with me just now," he explained to Anne.

"Between that and the servants' wages and Dr. Palmsey, it will eat up what you got at Eastleigh yesterday," Mrs. Tannie said.

"A pity. I had hoped to buy tiles from that blunt and pay off the merchants. We're so steeped in debt I'm reluctant to go into a shop. I wonder what else I can sell." His eyes wandered around the walls, hung with valuable paintings.

"Not the pictures, surely!" Anne exclaimed, alarmed to imagine things had come to such a pass.

"No, I'll go through the welter of things in Charlie's jewelry case. It's big as a shoebox, full of tiepins and rings and watch fobs. Good stuff—he had an eye for pretty gewgaws."

"Charles always dressed fine as a peacock," Mrs. Tannie said, but fondly.

Alex ignored the compliment. "We haven't done anything about our party, Anne. Have you decided what we should have first? The garden party, perhaps, while the weather is fine."

"It's a poor time to have a party, with money owing everywhere," Mrs. Tannie objected. "That stove in the kitchen is ready to topple over in a heap."

"You must know by now how things are done here," Alex said airily. "We do everything on tick."

"A garden party won't cost much, Aunt Tannie," Anne pointed out. She was looking forward to that party. "Let's make a list."

Tannie finished her tea and left them. "I'm surprised

Aunt Tannie didn't urge the party on us. She seems a bit stiff this morning," Alex said.

"Yes . . ."

"You sound as if you know something. What is it?"

"None of my business, really."

"Make it your business."

"Very well. It's not only your servants whose wages are in arrears. Charles told her he would give her a hundred a year when she came here. She was your papa's pensioner, but when she became housekeeper and substitute mother for the children as well, Charles promised her a wage. She tells me he never paid a sou."

"Good lord, why didn't she tell me? You mean all these years—never paid anything at all?"

"She bought what she required on credit."

"That comes to—something like five hundred pounds I owe her. Where am I to raise all this money?" He ran his fingers through his short hair worriedly. "I know how the government feels. I owe the whole world back wages."

"What about your rents, your income?"

"The rents are down more than a third, but I'll see what I can wring out of the bank."

"Alex, the income used to be ten thousand! Surely you can't be in financial trouble, *real* trouble, I mean."

"Not desperate trouble. A temporary shortage only. Penholme is mortgaged to the roof. Papa already had twenty thousand on it, and Charlie upped it another twenty. It's only worth fifty altogether. I don't know how he talked anyone into letting him have such a sum."

"Why would he need that much money?"

"Charles liked the best. I've often heard him say so. 'The best' doesn't come cheap. A pity he didn't carry that philosophy over to hiring a governess. Or getting the best rate on the mortgage, for that matter. He paid ten percent for the second mortgage.''

Anne sat, dumbfounded. "But if the rents are down and the mortgage up so high, it—it doesn't leave much. . . ." She did some rapid arithmetic and soon realized that Alex had less than half what she had supposed was needed to operate Penholme and all the other nonprofitable properties.

"Don't worry. I'll come around. Now about this party.''

She felt faint. "Why don't you wait a little, Alex? Business before pleasure.''

"I've waited a long time for this pleasure. A simple garden party doesn't seem too much to ask.'' The vehemence of his tone surprised her. She thought it even surprised him, and embarrassed him, for he soon pulled in his horns. "Perhaps you're right. I have to go to London, and Robin is itching to get to Sawburne.''

"Are you quite sure you can afford to give him Sawburne?''

"It's not mine; it's his, morally his. I'd like to give it to him soon. Like the rest of us, Robin has only one life to live. Mother insisted on buying Sawburne—for me, the second son. Rob's the second son now. I have no right to deprive him of it. I'm right about Sawburne, and you're right about the party. We can't afford it. Sensible Annie, what would we do without you?'' His smile was warm, despite the unhappy topic.

"Sink into a morass of parties and balls,'' she said.

"And debt. But it isn't hopeless, you know. I'll come around soon. We must be patient a little longer.'' He looked at her with an impatient expression—intent, questioning.

Anne felt as surely as she was sitting in his gold saloon that he was talking about marriage. It was a perfectly presumptuous thing to read into his innocent words, but when he reached out and patted her hand, she knew it was that and nothing else that he meant. His fingers ran over the opal ring she wore. She always wore it now. When he smiled softly, she knew exactly what was in his mind: I hope you will have a lovelier one, one day, to wear on the other finger. The atmosphere was so heavy she sought to lighten it.

"Thinking of taking my gift back and pawning it?" she asked.

"Not even close. Will you stay to lunch?"

"I don't want to leave Mama alone. I'll be going now."

He accompanied her to the stable. As he helped her onto Lady's back, he looked along all the empty stalls in the useless addition Charles had built and scowled.

"I'm driving over to Sawburne with Robin tomorrow," he said before she left. "We'll get an early start and be back by afternoon. I'll call around three or four, if that's all right."

"I'll give Mama the order and tell her to be home, with tea ready."

"It's *you* I'm coming to see, Duck," he said with an intimate, meaningful smile.

Anne's spirits soared as she cantered home through the flower-dappled meadow. She knew her mother wanted this match with Alex, and as a sort of daydream, she had often considered it. It would be a marvelous social coup, and of course extremely convenient. In these considerings, the only objection had been Alex himself. Cold, aloof Alex. How had she misread him so completely? Had she been so blinded by the dashing, reckless Charles that she'd never bothered to look—or had he changed?

From the moment he had bumped into her in the doorway of Rosedale and grabbed her in his arms to be welcomed home, he had seemed to view her as a lover. Almost as though he had come home and come to Rosedale with no other view than marrying her.

Chapter Seven

Anne's head was bent over her sewing as she sat in the saloon the next afternoon, awaiting the arrival of Alex and Robin. She hadn't paid much heed to fashion in the year and a half since Charles's death, but with Alex home, there would be a few small do's, and such gowns as she possessed were under revision for possible updating. The yellow silk on her lap was being enlivened with white lace and green ribbons. She wasn't sure whether it was an improvement or the opposite, but at least it was a change.

Her mind flew to that rapidly thinning bolt of creamy crepe in Mumbleton's drapery shop. She mentally balanced her dwindling allowance against absolutely necessary new gloves, a birthday present for Mama, a proper repair to her blue patent slippers (for the tacks piercing her toe rendered them nearly unwearable), and the white crepe. She had been deeply distressed to learn the crepe cost three guineas a yard. A daring straight gown was what she had in mind, and the pattern called for three yards. She had never paid such a sum as nine guineas for material in her life; it was a monstrous extravagance. With a little rearranging and careful cutting and omission of the shawl, two yards would do it. A little frown puckered her brow as she considered

71

this important matter. Intent on the solution, she was unaware of company. Alex and Robin had stabled the curricle and come in the back door.

"If you hate sewing as much as that Roman frown indicates, why do you do it?" Robin asked.

She looked up to see two handsome young men smiling at her. Both were decked out in fawn trousers and Hessians—city clothes, instead of their customary buckskins and top boots. Robin was undeniably the more handsome, but it was at Alex that she looked longer. A spontaneous smile of surprise lit her face.

"Because I hate appearing in public in antiquated outfits even more. This dear antique!" She held it up for their inspection. "You will recognize it, Robin, and possibly even you, Alex, have seen it before, for it's more than three years old." Robin came and took up the chair closest to her.

"You wore it to the last assembly before I left," Alex said promptly. "I didn't think it did you justice."

"You are kind. Charles was more outspoken. He told me it made me look bran-faced, and my complexion, you know, was always considered my redeeming feature." She noticed the little shadow of annoyance pass over Alex's face and regretted that unnecessary reference to Charles. "We have aged and mellowed together, this gown and I. We are now both approaching a sere and yellow condition that makes it suit me much better."

"Don't you think it time to retire the gown?" Alex asked. He looked rather pointedly at Robin, who ignored him. Rather than taking a chair farther away, Alex moved the gown and sat on the sofa by Anne.

She was perfectly aware of the small incident and felt a sense of gratification. "It has seen good and faithful service, but like Mrs. Dobbin, till a gift replaces it, it must

72

go on doing duty. And that is *not* a hint for a new gown, Lord Penholme!''

''I didn't mistake it for one. Even if it were, it would be a hint that must go unheeded. Rob and I are just back from Sawburne and have decided to declare ourselves bankrupt.''

This startling intelligence was accompanied by a rueful smile that bespoke hyperbole. ''You, too?'' Anne asked, shaking her head in commiseration. ''What we all ought to do is set up a shop of some sort. Mama claims it is the avaricious merchants who are making all the money these days. I believe she's right. The gown I covet would require a fortune. Three guineas a yard, they are charging for crepe nowadays. One would think it were gold or silver. Well, how bad is it at Sawburne?''

''Very bad,'' Alex answered soberly. ''In much the same state as Penholme. Mortgaged to the hilt, and the farms badly run-down. At least the merchants aren't getting up a rebellion against us.''

''Charles never lived there, so no bills have been run up,'' Robin explained. ''A few thousand should put me on my feet.''

''Is that all? Shake the pennies out of your piggy bank,'' Anne suggested.

''I did that a year ago to buy Babe a birthday present. There ain't any pennies in it, nor anywhere else either. We must be the *poorest* rich people in Hampshire.''

''You may well be,'' Anne sympathized, ''but Mama and I claim the title of the poorest *poor* people.''

''At least you have a trade. You can set up a cobbler's shop,'' Robin said.

''I'm too inept. My toe is pierced like a pincushion from the shoddy job I did on my own slippers. I'm after Mama to marry the butcher, but she favors the draper, I believe.

There, my thread is gone, and where will I ever find three pennies to buy a new spool?'' She set aside the gown with a sigh of relief and asked Cook to bring tea and call her mother down from the cheese room.

"Water will do, if you're short of tea," Alex suggested. Though he made a joke of it, there was an underlying sadness as he looked around the saloon. It wore the tired appearance not of neglect but of lack of money.

"No, no. We disregard our sad state and go on living like queens," Anne assured him. "Bread and tea every morning, a soup bone for lunch. And if there is no moon at night, we send the backhouse boy up to Penholme in the dark to steal eggs for next day's tea. You poor rich never miss them, I daresay."

"How did everybody get so *poor* all of a sudden?" Robin asked. He set his chin in his hands and frowned.

"You haven't been listening to me," Anne chided. "It is the merchants' fault. Old Anglin is rich as Croesus. He has two daughters, Robin. If you had your wits about you, you'd go into town and roll your eyes at one of them."

"The younger ain't half bad," Robin said with a quizzing smile.

"What's her dot?" Alex asked.

"Why, for a minor lord who will one day possibly own a heavily mortgaged and dilapidated farm, I expect he'd hand over a million or so," Anne said.

"No, for that price he'd expect me to take the elder antidote off his hands," Robin said, laughing.

Alex looked from one to the other as they joked. "It's gratifying to see such high spirits in these troubled times."

"It's breeding that accounts for it," Robin said.

"We laugh in the face of adversity and pretend to enjoy wearing threadbare clothes," Anne told him. "Anyone with a new bonnet each season is considered a parvenu. Mind

74

you, there aren't many such low types hereabouts. There's scarcely a jacket in the village with any nap left on it."

"Barring the merchants," Alex added.

"Well, I don't enjoy wearing boots three years old, and I'm sorry to hear you've given up cobbling, Annie," Robin said. "I was hoping you'd tack a new half sole on my top boots. The soles are so thin I can tell when I step on a coin whether it's heads or tails."

"Never mind whether it's heads or tails. Just bend over and put it in your pocket," Alex urged.

Anne turned to Alex. "You were going to alleviate some of the problems by selling your brother's jewelry. Have you done it?"

"No, Rob and I have sorted through it and have a load ready to take to Winchester. I ought to go to London, but we'll get a fair price in Winchester. We'll take it over tomorrow. Till I have some gold to disburse, I daren't show my face in Eastleigh."

"You never saw such gimcrack stuff, Annie," Robin said. "A gold toothpick, for instance. Now, why the deuce would anyone want a gold toothpick?"

"Just what I always wanted!" she exclaimed, laughing. Despite the nature of their conversation, she suddenly felt happy. It was having friends to share troubles that made them tolerable. "You must own that it would be the height of elegance to pull out a gold toothpick after our dinner of purloined eggs."

"And he had forty-five snuffboxes," Robin continued, eager to relate the list.

"That sounds a trifle excessive. I should think thirty would be enough. One for every day of the month. Especially when one considers that Charles hardly ever took snuff."

"Eleven watches—one of them a dandy Breguet. Sixteen

fobs, some of them quite valuable. Gold and jeweled, and the tiepins!''

"Forty-five?" Anne asked. "To match the snuffboxes, I mean."

"Not quite. Thirty, we counted."

"He was trying to economize, poor fellow."

"Oh, as to that, they are the most valuable pieces in the bunch. If they're genuine, that is. I cannot think the emerald is real, but two of the diamonds certainly are. One of them must be five or six carats, and there's a black pearl."

"You'll have to clean it up before you sell it," Anne advised.

"No, it's supposed to be black."

Alex listened to their nonsense and finally spoke. "She's pulling your leg, greenhorn."

"I never pull a gentleman's leg," Anne retaliated. "It sounds excessively vulgar. Have I not just been telling you what a pattern-card of breeding I am?"

"Sorry to hear it." Robin sighed. "I was counting on you to fix up these boots of mine."

"If you have no objection to tacks sticking in your toes, leave them with me. The charge will be nominal, for a friend."

"I'll tell you what I will do, if you don't mind, Alex," Robin said, "is get into Charlie's closets and dig myself out a new pair. He has dozens of them, and we are about the same size."

"We shall be paying for them, no doubt," Alex replied. "You must certainly feel free to wear them or anything else that fits you."

"I thought maybe you'd want them yourself," Robin said. "They'd be about your size, too."

"No, take anything you want," Alex repeated rather curtly.

"Anything?" Robin's eyes glowed with delight.

"Why not?"

"By Jove, I'll be the best-dressed pauper in the countryside. He has dozens of dandy jackets, and the waistcoats! A superb black evening outfit, too, and a sable-lined cape."

"There is your problem taken care of," Anne said. "I don't suppose he has a white crepe anything. I have been coveting a white crepe gown the past months."

"No, but he has half a dozen dressing gowns, all silk with fringed belts, and one with a bird of paradise on the back."

"Just a trifle gaudy for my taste," she said consideringly.

Mrs. Wickfield came in, bearing the tea tray, and the conversation came down to earth. She shook her head to hear of conditions at Sawburne and repeated that it was the merchants who were at fault. "The Anglins . . ." she said, preparing her tirade.

"Watch your words, Mama," Anne cautioned. "Robin is considering offering for the younger—or is it the elder, Robin? You might as well go for a million."

"I wouldn't be too civil to them, Robin," Mrs. Wickfield warned. "People like that—why, they might take it seriously."

"The girls are actually well-behaved," Robin objected. "Maggie and Marilla went to a ladies' seminary and might pass for ladies anywhere."

"Ah, but ladies in a new bonnet every season—parvenus," Anne chided. "Would they have the fortitude to be ladies in three-year-old silks?"

"Indeed they would not!" Mrs. Wickfield said sharply.

"I had tea with Mrs. Anglin at a church do, and she dunked her biscuit."

"Maggie don't dunk her biscuits," Robin defended.

"Robin, I hope you're not setting up a flirtation with Maggie Anglin," Anne exclaimed. "If it's only a fortune to bring Sawburne around that worries you, marry me. I have five thousand. That should do it, should it not, Alex?" Though the offer was not serious, she was displeased to hear Robin speak so hotly about Miss Maggie.

"More than do it," Alex agreed.

"Well, there you are, then," Anne said. "It isn't necessary to marry new money. Take me, and you'll get old, well-bred money. Tell him, Alex. You like giving orders."

"Not that order," he said, and slanted a smile at her. "Fine as well-bred money is, I cannot think five thousand old is finer than a million new."

"No, no, the elder daughter is going for a million. He cannot expect a sou over five hundred thousand for Maggie."

"Twenty-five thousand is what you would get. Something in that order," Mrs. Wickfield said.

"I ain't planning to marry her," Robin said, becoming angry. "But it's an idea, now that you mention it. He'd come down heavy for a title for her—sort of a title, Lady Robin. Of course, he'd come down a deal heavier to make her Lady Penholme."

Anne turned a sapient eye on Alex. "I trust you know your duty, Penholme."

"I begin to think it would take Anglin's fortune to keep me afloat. I notice you don't offer *me* your well-aged dowry, Annie."

"A paltry five thousand! It would be but a drop in the bucket to a man of your debts."

Mrs. Wickfield disliked to hear Alex's debts and Anglin's fortune discussed in the same conversation. She cleared her throat and said, "You could always sell the London mansion, Alex."

"Not if I can help it. It took my family six generations to build up their assets. I don't plan to preside at their disbursement."

"There's the Leicester hunting box—that is hardly ever used."

"It's gone," he said curtly.

"Gone where?" she asked, startled.

"Charles sold it before I left."

"Sold the Leicester place! I never heard about that." She exchanged a shocked, angry glance with her daughter.

"He needed the money," Alex said.

"What for?"

"To pay some debts."

"Deuce take it, I don't see that we must keep it a secret from Aunt Alice," Robin said to his brother. "He gambled it away. Owed three thousand to the moneylenders, and sold it three days before Alex left. That's why—"

"Never mind, Robin," Alex said sharply. "It's gone, but it will be the last property to leave this family if I can help it." He rose with a commanding glare at his brother. "Ladies, we'll leave you to your mending and cobbling and hope to see you tomorrow at Penholme. Come to tea. The moon is full tonight, so your backhouse boy will have poor foraging in the henhouse."

It was agreed, a time set, and an order given by Mrs. Wickfield that they would take their own gig, as day travel in it was pleasant.

While the gentlemen drove home, the elder burning Robin's ears for revealing Charlie's iniquity in selling the hunting box, Mrs. Wickfield turned a knowing eye on her daughter.

"That's why Alex left!"

"It seems like it."

"They had a fight, I wager. There was Alex looking after Penholme, trying to keep the place intact, while that bounder of a Charles was out squandering the family fortune. Selling the Leicester place! I can't believe it. And mortgaging everything else he could get his hands on. If the main estate weren't entailed, he'd have sold it up, too."

"He put another twenty thousand mortgage on it. What did he do with so much money?"

"Bought anything he took a fancy to. Gambled, showered it on his women friends, the gudgeon. What was your point in as well as refusing Alex, my lady?"

"Refusing him? Mama, we were joking. You might as well say I offered for Robin."

"Folks have a way of saying what they mean in the form of a joke, to see how it goes down. If he makes *that* joke again, I suggest you tell him he's welcome to your five thousand."

Anne smiled but was soon frowning again. "I wonder if Robin's joke about Maggie Anglin's fortune was said for the same reason."

"My dear, he'd never marry that vulgar merchant's daughter."

"Better he than Alex."

"Now, that is what you should have said! Though as I consider it, Anglin would not settle for such a little title as Robin's. He always buys the best. He'd be angling for the title of countess for his chit, if he should take into his head to look toward the Hall."

Anne's head turned slowly to her mother. She opened her lips, then closed them again. Alex had really not said a word against the Anglins. What he had said was that he could overlook their vulgarity, if the price was right. Did

80

he mean he could overlook it in a sister-in-law? Surely that was his meaning. Of course it was. It was pleasant to see Alex and Robin on such good terms, after a rough settling-in period. With two good men concentrating on the job of bringing order to Penholme, the future looked bright.

Chapter Eight

Anne knew as soon as she set foot in the door of Penholme the next afternoon that there was some excitement in the air. She saw it in Mrs. Tannie's smile as she greeted them at the door of the gold saloon, she heard it in the excited chatter of the rest of the family as they sat in groups talking, and most of all she felt it in the one long, meaningful look Alex cast on her when she entered. He wasn't quite smiling, but there was a happy excitement in his eyes. He looked as if—she hardly knew what. As if he wanted to take her into his arms and kiss her. He had never done anything of the sort, so how did she know? She just knew, that's all.

When she spoke to him, however, she gave no intimation of her powers of telepathy. "Why are you looking like the cat that swallowed the canary?" she asked. "Have you won a fortune at faro, I hope?"

"No, but I made a small fortune at Winchester."

"They liked the snuffboxes!"

"They were mad for them. Charlie *did* have good taste, to give him his due."

"I trust you mean to disburse your windfall profits with discretion," she said.

"They are disbursed."

"All of them! I begin to think we have another spend-thrift on the loose. Would it be encroaching to ask what sum you fell heir to?"

"Twenty-five hundred guineas."

"Oh, Alex! You're rich again." She beamed. It felt as though a heavy rock had fallen off her heart.

"I'm less steeped in debt. I paid Tannie her back wages and took care of the more pressing debts in the village. Oh, and paid the rector for his tedious sermons. I saved enough to buy a couple of yards of that inordinately expensive material your heart desires, if you're interested."

"Get thou behind me, Satan! I am only flesh and blood. Don't tempt me into such impropriety, Alex. I shall go through my own treasure box and see what I might pawn. I have a pretty good string of glass beads that I hardly ever wear, and a little cameo pin that is not so very chipped, only, of course, the clasp is broken."

"They ought to be worth a few hundred," he said.

"Is there such a demand for snuffboxes, then?"

"It was the tiepins that proved a boon. The large green stone was an emerald. There were a couple of diamonds in the lot and, of course, the black pearl."

"And the gold toothpick. What sum did it bring?"

"You didn't really think I'd sell it, when you always wanted one?" He removed the gold stick from his pocket and presented it to her with a ceremonious bow.

"Oh, thank you," she said, and stood looking at it uncertainly. "My, it's big, isn't it? It cannot be a lady's toothpick."

"I don't believe it's a toothpick at all, but for want of any rational conjecture, Robin has decided it must be one."

"Perhaps it's a spear for pickles," she suggested, hefting the spear, which was three inches in length and pointed at both ends. "But really, you know, just in case—I dislike to use another person's toothpick. I shall leave it in your safekeeping." She gave it back to Alex, who put it into his pocket with such a satisfied smile that she had to wonder why he'd offered it to her in the first place.

The twins, Bung and Willie, pelted forward to boast of the new suits ordered for them, real suits, with shirts and cravats just like a man's.

"And sleeves with three-inch hems on the cuffs," Alex added, "so I won't have to order new ones in six months."

"Children are so inconsiderate, they will just go on growing out of every stitch they own."

Babe came forward to grab Anne's hand and said in a confiding tone, "Alex is going to take me to Eastleigh and buy me new slippers. Blue patent ones, like yours, but I can't wear them."

"Very wise. Wearing slippers is hard on them."

"Except for church and parties."

"When you pull the sole off, you must bring them to Cousin Anne for mending. What did Loo get from the fortune? I see your brother has been busy getting rid of every penny of it."

"Loo's getting shoes, too, and we're getting a new governess. One that talks French."

"Chère moi! How exciting."

"I had to invent some excuse to be rid of Miss Pruner," Alex explained. "She doesn't speak French—or hardly proper English, for that matter. I've done as you suggested and made my presence felt in the schoolroom. After three complaining visits, she felt a strong urge to visit her mother. As her wedding is imminent, she shan't be returning. Fortunately, I had enough money to pay her off. I'll let the girls holiday till August, then find a suitable lady to replace her."

84

"Send Loo over to Rosedale if you want her to get started on French. Other than the subjunctive and irregular verbs, I'm quite a dab at it. It is a pity so many of the French verbs are irregular."

"You're busy enough, Anne. You're already teaching your backhouse boy and doing some of your own work around the house now."

"I see what it is. You think that only because I can't speak French myself I am in no position to teach another, but you're quite out. It would be an excellent way for me to learn it." She looked to the doorway and uttered a startled "Oh!" as Lord Robin strolled in, sporting an elegant blue coat of Bath cloth, a rose-sprigged waistcoat, fawn trousers, and shiny Hessians.

"Quite the tulip since he got into Charlie's wardrobe," Alex commented.

"That accounts for his grandeur. What a turn he gave me. He looks so terribly like Charles, doesn't he?" The words were out before she remembered Alex disliked that subject, especially in the way of approval. But it was impossible to act as though Charles had never existed. "I didn't notice it before, in his ordinary clothes. He's done something to his hair, too, hasn't he?"

"He went to a stylish barber in Winchester and got a Brutus do. All the crack."

"Very chic." As her eyes ran over this apparition, Robin finished his greeting to her mother and advanced to her.

He raised his hands and executed a mincing pirouette. "Just look. Don't touch!" he said in a mock-haughty tone.

"How can I be expected to keep my hands off such a dashing blade? You will be positively ravaged, Robin, if you go into society looking so irresistible."

"Not at all. I've developed a sneer to go with the outfit. Freezes 'em dead in their tracks. Tell her, Alex."

"He was turning every head in Winchester, I promise you," Alex agreed. "They hadn't seen such a popinjay there before. Mistook him for a dandy." If this was a posthumous jibe at Charles, Alex's smiling face didn't reveal it.

"This is only one of my lesser ensembles?" Robin warned her.

"For your lesser friends, such as I?" she quizzed.

"I'm introducing you to my new style by degrees. Wait till you see me rigged out in Charlie's black monkey suit for the assembly in Eastleigh. We really ought to have kept a diamond stud to do it justice. Weston, you know— the finest tailor in London. And once winter hits us, it'll be the sable-lined cape. I might go up to London and become Prinny's new adviser. He'll mistake me for the lord of the manor."

"You certainly look like him," Aunt Tannie said from across the room. "The late lord, I mean. You are the picture of Charles. Don't he look like him, Alex?"

It wasn't necessary for Alex to reply. Mrs. Tannie had come forward to examine the apparition more closely. "You nearly gave me an apoplexy when you came mincing in, fine as nine pence. Clothes make the man, eh?"

"A common misconception, ma'am," Robin told her. "These duds wouldn't look anywhere near so fine on a donkey or a pig. It's the man who makes the clothes."

"The clothes are in some danger of making this man into a jackass," Anne warned.

"Now that's just your jealousy speaking. You know once I go on the strut in this rig, the ladies will be all over me. You're afraid I won't have time for you."

"Cut to the quick!" she said, clutching melodramatically at her heart. "The day will come when those fine

Hessians, too, wear thin. Then we'll see you crawling back to your old friends, begging for a new half sole.''

"Don't hold your breath. I have half a dozen pairs as good as this. No, sir, I'm set till I manage to nab an heir-ess.''

"You might look higher than Miss Maggie Anglin if this is the style you mean to present,'' Aunt Tannie suggested.

Impatient with this subject, Alex said, "Did we tell you Rosalie and Exmore are coming to visit tomorrow? My return is the reason given, but I suspect it was timed to coincide with the spring assembly. You ladies must come to dinner while they're with us.''

"You must all come to Rosedale, too,'' Mrs. Wickfield said. "We haven't done a thing to welcome you home, Alex.''

"No, no. You can't be entertaining with no help,'' he said quickly.

"We still have Cook.''

"And our backhouse boy to raid your poultry house for food,'' Anne added.

"Why, we can send down a batch of servants to lend you a hand,'' Aunt Tannie offered. "The crew here seems to keep multiplying. As soon as a footman marries, he brings his wife to work, and the wife has a sister, and before you know it, we've got a whole new family under-foot.''

"Why don't you let some of them go?'' Mrs. Wickfield asked.

"Jobs are scarce,'' Alex said vaguely.

"So is money, and servants must be paid.''

"They're not paid much. I was embarrassed to hand them their wages. Of course, they get their room and board. Food at least is plentiful. How do you refuse a job to one of your own tenant farmers' girls?''

Aunt Tannie turned a knowing eye on him. "That means you've hired Mollie Prawne, I suppose?"

Alex shrugged. "What could I do? Prawne has six children at home to feed. They look like skeletons. She'll only be getting twenty pounds a year."

"Why, *we* could afford her," Mrs. Wickfield said. "Our Mary demanded thirty-five, which is why we had to let her go."

Alex looked a question at Anne. "Could you afford Mollie?"

"Mama is in charge of the big finances. I only have to worry about my own two hundred and fifty a year. If she says she can afford her, goodness knows we could use her."

It was arranged on the spot between Alex and Mrs. Wickfield, and without a word to say about it, Mollie Prawne was exchanged.

Penholme had indicated that eating with the children was an experience not to be repeated, but when high tea was served, the twins offered their arms to their sisters, and the whole family went to the dining room. The youngsters had received a stiff lecture that they were to be seen and not heard. They behaved well for ten minutes, but then their patience gave out and the remainder of the meal was as boisterous as before. There was no talk of the boys becoming soldiers, however. Bung had decided that he would be Prime Minister, while Willie spoke of riding the horses at Astley's Circus.

Aunt Tannie bemoaned the state of the blue suite, saying it was too bad they hadn't time to get it fixed up before Rosalie's arrival.

"Rosalie is family," Alex said. "We don't have to put on airs for her. Exmore is a man of the world. It will not be news to him that our pockets are to let. I daresay it's buzzed all over London by now. I must get up to London very soon and see just how I stand with creditors there."

"Get yourself some new jackets while you're in town," Aunt Tannie suggested.

Alex said nothing, but he looked interested. It was only natural that a young bachelor would want a new set of clothing after three years in uniform, and Anne assumed that if the finances were in order, he would return as fine as Robin.

Though it was only high tea that was served, it was served in the dining room, and the gentlemen remained behind for port. When they rejoined the ladies, Robin went to sit beside Anne. It was natural he should choose the younger lady, but on this occasion she rather wished he had not. Especially when Alex gave a dissatisfied look at them and went to join Aunt Tannie and her mother.

Robin immediately began an amusing exposition on the selling of Charlie's effects, and before long she was laughing to hear how Alex had scooped the whole lot back into the box when the man, mistaking them for a pair of flats, had offered a mere thousand pounds.

"I believe he thought we'd pinched the stuff," Robin rattled on. "You should have seen Alex get on his high ropes. Sounded for the world like Papa in a huff. 'The Penholmes of Penholme Hall are not accustomed to haggling. We ought to have taken these few trifles to Sotheby's,' he said. That made the old fellow look sharp, I can tell you. He stuck his loupe in his eye, and it nearly fell out from shock when he ogled the emerald tie stud. Jove, I bet Alex wished he could have kept it."

"He was never one for dolling himself up in jewels and finery."

"He never had the chance, had he? He's a Penholme, you know. There's a streak of the peacock in us all, no denying. He'd have decked himself out if he'd ever had two pennies to rub together. He always had to wear Charlie's reach-me-downs. He said, when I asked why he didn't grab himself a new pair of boots from Charlie's lot, that he'd felt the pinch of Charlie's boots for the last time. Said it in a bitter way, though he tried to hide his feelings.''

''Your mother was always fond of Alex. Could she not have done something for him?''

''She did the best thing, as it turns out. Set aside what monies she could keep her hands on and left it to Alex when she died. It was all that allowed him to buy his commission and outfit himself for the army. Charlie wouldn't give him a penny, after Alex running Penholme for him for eighteen months. Lord, what a time it was. A fight every time Charlie deigned to come home. He'd rip up at Alex for the dwindling income, and Alex would shout at him that he needed more money to do this and that about the place. But in the end, Charlie could always turn Alex up sweet. Tell him he couldn't get on without him. He'd give him the money next quarter or next year or what have you. Charlie had a lot of charm. Maybe too much, but in the end, Alex finally saw through him.''

''He left because of Charlie's selling the Leicester place, you mentioned.''

''The groundwork was set before that. Alex was driven to his wits' end. He said there was no point his trying to hold things together if Charlie was determined to put us all in the poorhouse. He didn't even have the decency to tell Alex he'd sold the Leicester place. Alex learned it from his agent and thought at last that he was going to get money to handle matters here, but it turned out it was only to pay gambling debts. He saw he'd have to make his own way in the world, for it was clear as a peddler's pikestaff by then that Charlie had no intention of turning Sawburne over to him. Alex even felt that the Hall might be lost in the long run, and—oh, you had to be there, Annie. I think Alex felt he had to build up something to look after the family, a career for himself, in case the worst happened. Mind you, he didn't tell me that in so many words, but he was really the one we looked to as a father. He didn't actually say so. He didn't say much, really. Well, he couldn't. He was demmed near bawling when he said good-bye to me, if you want the truth. You know how his jaw and throat muscles kind of clutch into a knot when he's beyond words.''

Anne listened reluctantly, not wanting to believe, but Robin's forthright story had to be true. Every fact substantiated it. Her wonderful hero, her beloved, shining Charles, was a miserable, selfish fool. How could she have been so unseeing? How had she admired Charles and his "charm," which was just another word for not caring, for selfishness? Worse, how had she never appreciated that quiet Alex was the real man of the family, the master—in all but authority. How different things would have been had he been born the elder son. But he was the eldest son now. It wasn't too late.

"We aren't usually excluded from family gossip at Rosedale. How does it come no one told us about this?''

"Folks like to hide their troubles, I suppose. Rosedale was like an oasis, Annie. It was nice to go there and just get away from the squabbling. Then Alex left after ringing such a peal over Charlie, I still hear it in my sleep sometimes. Irresponsible, he called him. Not worthy to bear the title of Penholme. If the girls ended up on the street and the boys in Newgate, it was on Charlie's head. His rant seemed to have some good effect, for a while. Charlie talked about trying to bring himself around, but as you can see, nothing came of it. He fell in with the racing set and squandered whatever more he could get his hands on. You were well out of it, I can tell you. Of course, Papa had already made inroads on the estate before Charlie took over. It ain't fair to put the whole of it in Charlie's dish.''

They finished talking and sat silent for a moment while Anne absorbed all this unknown background. She looked up to see Alex gazing at her. He rose and came toward them. ''What has put you two in the hips?'' he asked. ''You look as though you're in attendance at a wake. Don't you know a gentleman is supposed to entertain a lady, Robin?''

''Robin has made himself extremely interesting,'' she said.

''It would be his resemblance to his late brother that accounts for it, no doubt.''

''Only a superficial resemblance,'' Robin said, displeased with the comparison, and Anne now understood why.

''Sit down,'' she said to Alex.

''I was about to, but I had the feeling I might be *de trop* at this tête-à-tête.''

''No, I am the one who is *de trop,*'' Robin said. He rose with a smile and a gallant bow and went to tease Loo.

''Now, where did he get that idea?'' Alex asked.

''Your sneer might have led him to it, or perhaps it was the way you pulled him out of his chair. Robin is sensitive to hints.''

Alex smiled and took up the vacant seat. ''What were you two talking about?''

''The past,'' she said, studying him. It wasn't only the Peninsula that had etched those lines in his forehead. They must have already begun to invade before he had left. What a horrible time Charles had led the family, and he always so charming and cheerful in public.

"That's French for Charlie, I assume."

"You're worse at the language than I am. Come down to Rosedale with Loo and we'll all learn the bongjaw together. I believe the French call the past *le passé.*"

Then it cannot refer to Charles. Nothing *passé* about him."

"Alex, why didn't you tell me. . . ." She stopped, realizing that a party was not the time or place for a serious discussion.

Alex ignored her half question. He looked across the room, then turned back in a moment with a whole new expression on his face. He was polite and smiling. "How are you and Lady getting along?"

"Famously. Lady and I have reached a better understanding than a certain gentleman and I. How long will it be till you can ride? Does your wound still bother you much?"

"Only when I exert it. It will be a few weeks yet before I can ride. I'm looking forward to riding with you."

He was willing to discuss the present and the future as agreeably as anyone could wish, but any slight reference to the past, and especially Charlie, closed him up like a clam.

Anne and her mother left before dark settled in. Alex said he would send word over to them when Rosalie arrived. When Anne lay in her bed, she reviewed her conversation with Robin—all those startling revelations about Charles and Alex. She regretted all the unkind things she had said. She no longer wondered that Alex occasionally let fall a gibe against Charles; she only wondered that he didn't shout from the rooftops what he had had to put up with.

Charles had used her badly, too, leading her on just enough to keep her interest alive, when he had no intention of marrying her. If it weren't for that, she might have fallen in love with Alex ages ago. But he was home now, and Charles was gone. It wasn't too late. It was time for them both to let go of old passions, old loves, and old enmities and get on with the future.

Chapter Nine

It was Mollie Prawne and not a footboy who brought news of Rosalie and Exmore's arrival the next day. She was sent down in a gig from Penholme just after lunch and delivered her precious news while she bobbed a curtsy to her new mistress. The Wickfields were requested to go up to the Hall as soon as it was convenient, but with a new servant to be shown her duties and her way around the house, "convenient" was not very soon.

Once Mollie was settled in, Anne and Mrs. Wickfield made their grandest toilette, knowing that even their grandest was inadequate to impress a fashionable young duchess with an eye that could spot a remodeled gown at sixty paces. Both ladies admitted to feeling foolish setting forth in a gig in broad daylight, rigged out in their evening dresses, but the invitation included dinner, so it was either that or darting home to change in a few hours.

The duchess sat alone with Aunt Tannie when the Wickfields arrived. Rosalie was as beautiful and trim as when she had been a maiden, in spite of her having borne two children. Her black hair was twisted in a Grecian knot, an elegant topping for her splendid rose gown. She was of the same strain as Charles and Robin, with the same large and lustrous blue eyes, heavily fringed with black lashes. She made her cousins welcome and even granted Mrs. Wickfield the honor of rising upon her entrance. As she did so, her knowledgeable eyes ran over Anne's well-worn yellow gown. Really, the girl was hopeless!

"Dear Anne!" She smiled as she enclosed her cousin in a perfumed embrace. "How good to see you again. Isn't it wonderful to have Alex back home, safe and sound? Hasn't he grown thin, though? I've been teasing him this past hour for not eating properly in Spain. But you know Alex—he was always so fussy about his beefsteak being done just right. I scarcely recognized him."

Seats were taken, and conversation became general but mostly monopolized by the verbose duchess. "I could strangle Alex for not stopping off to see us on his way through London. I would love to have shown him off. However, he says he didn't know we were there. Imagine not knowing we were in London at the height of the Season! Where did he *think* we'd be?"

"We hadn't heard from you in a while, Rose," Aunt Tannie apologized. "We sent notes off to your London address and your country place, to make sure you got word immediately."

"It was a miracle I got your note. I was half packed to dart to Brighton for the weekend, for Exmore's uncle has a home there, you must know, right on Marine Parade. He begs us to spend time with him. We are missing a very fine ball in London tonight—the Castlereaghs—and the assembly at Almack's, not that *it* is worth worrying about. It is only good for finding a parti. I shall make sure to take Alex when he comes to town."

"How is Exmore?" Mrs. Wickfield asked when the duchess stopped to draw breath.

"In sterling health. He's out walking with Alex this minute. Nothing ever bothers him. I have had shortness of breath often the past month, but Exmore has the constitution of a horse. And the children take after their papa." She expatiated for several minutes on the precocity of her offspring, till her roving eye chanced to fall on Babe, which gave her chatter a new turn.

"What a little lady you are become, eh? You'll be coming to Rosalie to be presented one of these days."

"Loo will be there a good while before her," Aunt Tannie mentioned.

Loo was reaching the awkward age. She did not look nearly so appealing as Babe, which was held to account for her being ignored. Babe was allowed to sit at Rosalie's daintily shod foot and play with the flounce of her gown. There was, in fact, a better reason, but it was not generally known that Aunt Lucretia was on the point of dying and had mentioned Babe as being one of the recipients of her estate.

The country ladies had been put in touch with all the latest fashions at court and much of the gossip concerning people totally unknown to them before the gentlemen came in. They were dusty from their walk and had to change before joining the ladies. Exmore, the visitor, received the first attention of them all. He was not handsome and not particularly interesting, certainly not at all amusing, but he was Rosalie's ducal husband, and so all the ladies except his wife made a fuss over him.

Rosalie turned her flashing eye on Alex. "When are you coming to London to visit us? I've been bragging to the whole world that the hero of the Peninsular Campaign is my brother."

"I'm no hero," Alex objected.

"You are a slow top, Alex. I never saw your name in the list of honors. And came home only a major, after a year and a half. I swear if it had been Charlie, he'd be a general.''

"I'm not Charlie. And I shan't be visiting you, I'm afraid. I am very busy about the estate. I must make a short visit to the city, but I don't plan to make a social occasion of it.''

"But you'll come to dinner!'' Rosalie exclaimed.

"Certainly, but don't turn it into a party on my account.''

"You won't want to be seen till you get some decent jackets,'' Rosalie agreed mindlessly. Then her eye chanced to fall on Robin, and she went into ecstasies of delight. "Now, there is a lad I should be proud to have at my table. My, what a menace to civilization. Look at that jacket, Exmore. Why can't you look like that?''

How a stubby gentleman pushing forty with narrow shoulders and sandy hair was expected to accomplish this miracle did not occur to her.

"Heh-heh, a dashed handsome young fellow he has grown into.'' Exmore smiled.

"I can't afford Robin's tailor,'' Alex said.

"Not in the suds, I hope,'' Rosalie said swiftly.

"We're having tough sledding,'' he admitted. Rosalie and Exmore exchanged a quick glance, but nothing more was said.

Rosalie embarked on another round of gossip. "Exmore—dear Bertie—has bought me a new phaeton, if you please. He says I am a shocking poor ship and insists on accompanying me in the park. What a quiz we look, man and wife tooling through Hyde Park together. We go in the morning, when no one is there.''

"You'd look stranger with some other man by your side,'' Alex said. His sister stared at his antiquated notions.

"We've had gas put in the London house,'' Exmore

offered. "It's the coming thing. Gives a very good light, much brighter than candles. Bright as daylight."

"It sounds dangerous," Mrs. Tannie said with a shiver.

"We are very worried about poor Aunt Lucretia. She is not at all well" was Rosalie's next remark, uttered with a bright eye that belied her concern. "Seventy-five, of course, it is only to be expected. Shall I tell them, Bertie?"

"It ain't a secret, so far as I know."

"I'll tell you, then, but don't dare ask me how I know. Our solicitor, McDougall, is her man as well, and he let it slip. She is leaving some money to Babe." Babe's curls were rumpled affectionately at this news.

"How much?" Babe asked. "I hope it's a guinea. I want a new bridle."

Rosalie laughed gaily at such unimaginative desires. "More than that, Goosie."

Alex made no effort to conceal his interest. "How much is it?" he asked hopefully.

"Ten thousand pounds!" Rosalie announced, and laughed in pure joy at the sound of the words.

Loo took instant offense. "Why isn't she leaving *me* any?"

"Because she was the youngest daughter herself, and feels they are slighted. She's leaving the same to all her youngest great-nieces. How I wish I were the youngest." Rosalie sighed.

There was general rejoicing at this news, and Babe was heartily congratulated. "Very wise," Alex approved. "The youngest, and especially the girls, fare badly. Leave it to Lucretia—she was always a sound and sensible old lady. I daresay it would be a bit previous of me to write and thank her, as we haven't heard officially yet."

"It would be utterly farouche!" Rosalie objected. "But as you and the old lady always got on well, you must call on her when you're in London. Wear your regimentals. She has a soft spot for a uniform. It might put a new heir in her head."

"That would be because her husband was a soldier," Mrs. Wickfield mentioned.

"Was he?" Rosalie asked. "Fancy that. I often wondered who the ugly old fellow in the painting by her bed was. I hope I didn't twit her about him."

"My uniforms are put away in camphor," Alex said.

"Then get them out and air them!" Rosalie said, laughing.

"I'm no longer in the army. I've sold out."

"Lud, what does that matter? She'll never know the difference. What a simpleton you are, Alex. I swear none of you knows how to manage here since I left."

"I approve of Aunt Lucretia's manner of leaving her fortune. I won't try to turn her up sweet by playing on her sympathy."

"I begin to understand why you remained a major," Rosalie snipped. "You just said you were having tough times here."

"We are, but I'll take care of it."

"I hope you do it in a hurry, for I might as well get to the point at once, Alex. . . ."

He mistrusted that pious look on Rosalie's face. "What point?"

"Exmore wants to speak to you about that three thousand pounds you owe him." She leveled a commanding stare at Exmore.

Alex's face went perfectly blank. "I don't understand. I borrowed nothing from Exmore." He looked a question at his brother-in-law.

"No, no, it wasn't Alex, Rosie. We'll discuss it later."

"No, tell me now," Alex demanded.

It was typical of the Penholmes that a matter of this nature be discussed in front of everyone—guests, children, and all.

"The thing is," Exmore began reluctantly, "Charles borrowed three thousand from me six months before he died. He'd joined the Jockey Club, you recall—"

"I heard nothing about it. He didn't write to me at all."

"He never even told *me*," Robin said, offended at having been left out of this secret, which would have been of consuming interest to him.

"Well, he did it anyhow," Exmore continued. "He was planning to train a filly for the Derby—bought a flashy piece of horseflesh from Alvanley and gave it to the Croker brothers to train, but then he died before it ever ran, and the Crokers kept it as payment for stabling fees and training fees and so on."

"Oh, lord," Alex said. It was only a sigh, but his feelings were easy to read from his dejected face and sagging shoulders.

"And he never even paid the interest," Rosalie added.

"He was dead, Rose," her husband reminded her.

"It comes to close to four thousand now," Rose continued. "He gave Bertie a note at ten percent two years ago, and with the high cost of everything nowadays, we could use the money."

"Rosie, I can't pay it right away," Alex said with a worried frown. "I've been selling everything that isn't nailed down to pay back wages and pay off the local merchants. Ten percent! Isn't that a bit steep? I mean, within the family."

"I don't suppose you wanted your own brother running to the cent percenters!" she riposted. "It's your duty, Alex. Your income is ten thousand a year."

"No, it isn't! It's down to six with the way things have

101

been mismanaged, and everything mortgaged to the roof. Penholme, Sawburne . . .''

"And Charlie sold the Leicester place, of course," Rosalie added. "Well, you can always sell the London house. You won't use it much anyway, if I know you."

"It begins to look as though I'll have to sell it," he said reluctantly. As they all watched, his reluctance stiffened to opposition. "I won't, though."

"If you can pay everyone else, you can pay the family," Rosalie said, a martial fire burning in her eyes.

"You can have my money, Alex," Babe said trustingly. Rosalie nodded in approval.

"Don't be foolish," Alex said. "That's yours. It begins to look as though it's all you can ever depend on, so you'd best hang on to it."

"You will be her guardian," Rosalie pointed out.

"Rosalie! You surely don't expect me to steal Babe's inheritance to pay Exmore!"

Exmore sat embarrassed, for he was not yet accustomed to the Penholmes' blunt way of dragging all the dirty linen into the middle of the saloon.

"I didn't say steal," Rosalie countered. "Borrow it. Pay her interest."

"With what money do I repay her? We're holding on here by our fingernails. And anyway, Lucretia isn't dead yet. Whatever possessed you to lend Charles such a sum? You might have known he'd squander it."

"He was making up to Sylvia Mapleton at the time. She has a huge dowry and is very horsey. It seemed like a good idea."

"He only said that to get the money out of you," Alex said bitterly.

"That's not true. They were always together."

"I don't see why Alex should be hobbled with Charlie's debts," Robin said.

Rosalie gave him a vastly superior look. "It is a matter of honor, Robin dear. When you're older, you'll understand."

"I understand well enough you're dunning Alex for his brother's debts. Charlie was *your* brother, too. *You* take the loss."

"Shut up, you insufferable gas bag!" she shouted, all elegance forgotten.

Alex looked interested at his brother's idea, and Rosalie spoke on to settle the matter. "He borrowed it as Lord Penholme, you see, and now Alex is Lord Penholme, so the debt, like the title and estate, devolve upon him. I'm quite sure any solicitor would agree with me," she said brightly.

Exmore made a sound of disagreeing. "We don't intend to sue," he said.

Alex turned to Exmore. "How badly do you need the money?"

"I don't want to cause you any trouble, Penholme."

"Bertie!" Rosalie rapped out in a stern voice. "The fact of the matter is, we had hoped to take it back with us this week. Bertie's uncle usually gives us a couple of thousand every year, and we have come to depend on it, but he is cutting back, as everyone is, and tells us not to expect it this year. We have already spent it. The gas lighting and my new phaeton, and everything so wretchedly dear."

"Just when I thought I was coming around," Alex said grimly, but he shouldered this new responsibility. "I'll see what I can do. I'll try to raise it somehow within the next few weeks." He concluded that he must mortgage the London house, much as he disliked to, with all the other mortgages hanging over his head. How could he possibly pay

103

them all? He would have to rent the town house and let the rents pay off the mortgage. He felt as if an ocean of debt were engulfing him, leaving him gasping for air.

"Just how bad is it?" Rosalie asked.

"Very bad," he said. He went on to outline the financial chaos, and she nodded consideringly. She was not intelligent but had an animal cunning that found a solution before he finished.

"What you must do is come to London and marry yourself an heiress. Don't sell the London house. Open it up and throw a party."

"Are you insane? I can't afford to have the knocker screwed on, let alone staff the place and throw a party."

"Do it on tick. There aren't many handsome young earls on the market—a hero, to boot. A pity you sold out, or you could wear your uniform. There's an excellent crop of heiresses this year. The moneylenders are very considerate toward eligible lords."

"Don't be foolish," he said curtly.

"It is you who are being foolish. How else are you to come around? You're twenty-seven, Alex. It's time you were thinking of settling down. You've had your little fling, a spot of travel to foreign spots."

Alex just flickered a glance in Anne's direction, but Rosalie's lynxlike eyes saw it. She knew Alex used to be fond of Anne years ago but thought he had gotten over that when he left. Indeed, she always assumed it was Annie's rejection of his offer that sent him to Spain. No doubt Anne would accept now that Alex was Lord Penholme.

"I think it is a positive duty," she said piously, and looked around the room for support. "You have the twins and the girls to consider, to say nothing of Robin."

"He's giving me Sawburne," Robin said.

"Giving away estates—my, that doesn't sound like a poor man!"

"It's mortgaged," Robin said.

"And you get the mortgage to go with it, dear?"

"Yes, the mortgage to go with it! Alex had enough to worry about with the shambles Charlie made of everything. I'll bring Sawburne around myself. I can do it."

"Charles never could."

"He might have if you and others like you weren't so foolish as to go lending him money to toss around as though it were water. I don't think Alex is legally bound to pay. I bet you couldn't collect it in a court of law."

"That's enough, Rob," Alex said in a quelling voice. "Exmore lent the money in good faith and will be paid. Let's have done with this discussion."

And they were done with it. From a heated argument they soon sailed into a perfectly amiable discussion of plans for coming events: the assembly at Eastleigh, the garden party in the evanescent future, Babe's inheritance. By the time dinner was called, there wasn't a frown on any face, but there were plans a-plenty in every head. Alex worried over how he would juggle all his bills, Exmore pondered how to proceed without touching Alex for payment at this time, and Anne worried that Alex wasn't out of the basket yet. Rosalie mistrusted the way Alex directed his attention to Anne Wickfield. There was no counting on him to do the proper thing, but Anne was always a sensible girl. The position must be brought most forcefully to her attention. With this end in view, she chose a place at table beside Anne.

"I was speaking to Cousin Florian the other day, Anne," she began. "He's growing into a handsome fellow. Has he been down to Rosedale recently to look over his inheritance?"

"Not recently. We see him perhaps once a year. Mama has life tenancy, you know."

"Yes, but it will all be Florian's one day. How old is he now?"

"He must be eighteen or nineteen."

"Ah, he looks older. And you are twenty-one now, eh? All grown-up and looking about for a match, I daresay."

"I'm twenty-two," Anne replied.

"You still seem like a girl to me, an old married lady with two babes in the nursery. We are all getting on, are we not? After Alex is settled, I daresay you'll be the next one to marry, Anne. Alex must marry money, of course, the way things stand at present."

Anne stirred in discomfort, hardly knowing what to say. "He must do something to bring his affairs into order," she agree.

Rosalie's handsome eyes narrowed dangerously. "Oh, a good marriage—it is the only solution!"

"There is usually more than one solution to any problem, however complex," Anne replied, so coldly that Rosalie desisted and complimented Anne on her gold gown, which she had always like so much, and Anne must be fond of it, too, as she was still wearing it.

After the ladies retired to the gold saloon, the gentlemen remained at their port for longer than usual. Exmore liked his port very well, but eventually the impatient jiggling of Robin got through to him, and they all went along to the saloon.

Alex made a point of leading the group and took up the seat beside Anne before his brother could beat him to it. "What was Rosie saying to get your dander up at dinner?" he asked.

"She has turned matchmaker and is hinting me in Cousin Florian's direction."

"Florian? He's only a child."

"He's nearly twenty, and apparently looks older." A bark of laughter greeted this. "As she is lining up an heiress for you, I agree she might do better than a Bartholomew baby for me."

"Shall we tell her to butt out, or shall we let her prate on?"

"Till you see your way clear to repaying Exmore, I think the phrase 'butt out' had best be suppressed."

His brow furrowed, and he put a hand to his head in a troubled way to rub it. "I'll pay them, somehow."

"It's a pity she had gas light installed, and got a new phaeton when . . ."

"She didn't know how we were situated here. It's not Rosalie's fault," he said forgivingly. "Exmore was very good about it. He told me not to worry, not to do anything desperate, but of course he must be paid as soon as possible if they need the money."

"Oh, Alex, how badly can they need it? They look so prosperous."

"So do we," he said, and looked around the sumptuous saloon, where fine old furnishings, carpets, and paintings lent an air of opulence. "Who'd ever think to look at this room of people that we can't raise a penny among us?" His eyes turned to Anne, and his expression softened to a smile. "But really, I don't mind. I'm even becoming attached to your old gold silk gown. I was wrong and ungallant to suggest it didn't do you justice."

"No, Alex, you are ungallant to suggest it *does* do me justice. I would look much better in the white crepe, and one of these years I shall have it. About the time white crepe goes out of style, I expect. They always lower the price then."

"You look fine to me, Annie," he said, but his warm eyes said a great deal more.

Something in their attitude, leaning toward each other and smiling, alerted Rosalie to imminent danger. She catapulted herself forward to join them. "I've been racking my brain and have come up with the very heiress for you, Alex," she said brightly while darting suspicious looks from one to the other.

"Have you, Rosie?" he answered playfully. "I appreciate your concern but I think I have come up with an heiress of my own."

"Who?"

"A local lady. I'll let you know as soon as things are settled."

He didn't look at Anne, nor she at him, but a tension in the air spoke clearly of his meaning.

"But who is she?" Rosalie insisted. "What is her dowry?"

"Her dowry is not great, but she's an excellent manager."

"Surely not Miss Peoples! You can't mean Squire Peoples's girl, with only ten thousand. Why, a baronet is worth ten thousand. You must not settle for a penny less than twenty-five."

Alex's lips moved unsteadily. "It is not Miss Peoples's ten thousand I have in mind."

"I am relieved to hear it, for you will need much more than that."

"Yes, sis, and now that you've discovered I am all set, you can get back to Robin and find an heiress for him."

"That will present no problem. My, how he has blossomed. I bet you Sylvia Mapleton would give her eyeteeth for him. She was crazy about Charlie, and really they are as like as peas in a pod."

"Why don't you suggest it to him?" Alex asked.

"I shall, never fear. And I'll find a man for you, too, Anne."

"I thought you had settled on a boy for her," Alex said blandly.

Rosalie laughed, but mirthlessly. "You've been telling Alex what I said about Florian. Perhaps he is a little young, but I'll keep you in mind and see what I can do when I get back to London."

"You know, if I didn't owe you so much money, Rosalie, I'd tell you to butt out of our affairs," Alex said with a perfectly charming smile.

"Would you, Alex?" She smiled back. "But you *do* owe us nearly four thousand pounds, so I'll just go on butting away." She leaned back in her chair, determined to do exactly as she said, and with a mutual smile that worried her considerably, Anne and Alex relaxed, too, and let her butt away.

Before leaving, Mrs. Wickfield invited the whole party to tea the next day. There was some discussion as to who was included in the group. Everyone from Babe to Aunt Tannie was invited, but between Alex's insistence that such a party was too large and Tannie's suggestion that they take the girls but not the twins and Anne's complaint that the twins would be in the boughs for weeks if they were left out, nothing was definite.

The hostess fell into that morass of uncertainty that usually results when trying to assemble a party of indeterminate size. "Bring them all" was her parting command, but the echo of Alex's—"No, no, the children will remain home"—left some doubt. It was of cold ham and desserts the ladies spoke as they drove home in Penholme's closed carriage, with their own gig following.

More important matters had to wait till later for consideration, when Anne was in bed. Her love for Charles had dwindled over the months since his death. Really, she had loved only a memory for some time now, and learning the truth about him had soured even the memories, but it was of Charles that she thought that night. A charming wastrel who had wasted her youth, along with his family's fortune. And now it began to look as though his evil lived after him, ruining her chances and Alex's.

Chapter Ten

The Wickfields were no sooner seated at breakfast the next morning than the cook began sending messages up to them via Mollie Prawne. First they were told that a brace of fowl had been sent down from Penholme, and should she prepare them for tea, as a different menu had been settled on earlier?

"We had better, for likely as not the children will come, and they will like the fowl. Yes, tell Cook to go ahead and prepare the fowl as well as the ham."

Next it was a basket of fruit from Penholme's pinery, and what were the plans for it? It, too, was to be prepared and arranged to form an edible centerpiece for the table. When breakfast was finished and the ladies had begun the chore of readying the house for a visit from Londoners, for all this fuss and bother was only to impress the Exmores, a head of cheese and two quarts of cream were delivered. There was a note addressed to Miss Wickfield stuck into the basket, which she opened with some impatience at their benefactor.

It read: "Dear Duck: To save your backhouse boy his forays up the hill, pray tell me if there is anything you require for this afternoon. Your obedient servant, P."

She smiled and scrawled off a reply on the back of the same paper. "Dear Obedient: We require guests, as many as possible, with large appetites to consume the meal you have sent. A."

Alex always liked to include the children in any treat, and after reading her note, he issued the order that the children were to be dressed up to attend. Exmore's carriage and his were required to haul such a number of people. When Rosalie entered the saloon, she immediately began berating Alex for his thoughtlessness.

"Whoever heard of bringing children along to a grown-up party? Aunt Alice, I apologize on behalf of this brutish brother of mine."

"We're glad to have them."

Certainly the children were happy to be there. Nor were they much bother, for it was only afternoon, and they soon ran outdoors to amuse themselves in the sunshine. When they had left, Rosalie looked around to see how the place was holding up. She hadn't been to visit the Wickfields since Alex's departure three years before. Nothing had changed. The same carpets, same draperies, not a chair recovered or a new bibelot added to the room. She liked to be always changing and improving her own surroundings.

"Have you seen the lovely new Carlton House tables they are using in London?" she asked. "Really desks, with dozens of little drawers. So sweet. Bertie got me one for my study. One of them would look good in this room, Auntie—just there between the windows."

"We're not up to all the new rigs," Mrs. Wickfield told her. "We have the old Kent table desk in the study that we use for our writing."

"I remember it, but these new desks are much more elegant. Not great, heavy things like those of Kent."

"It would be out of place here. The furnishings are all old and heavy."

"The Sheraton chairs are not bad. Covered with some nice new bright material, they would smarten you up."

"The way of it is, if you go putting one new thing into a room, it makes everything else show its age," Mrs. Wickfield said resignedly.

"That's perfectly true," Rosalie agreed. "When I got my new Carlton House table, I had to redo the walls, for it didn't stand out against the old brown paper. I had them redone in yellow silk. It looks lovely."

She then turned to Anne. "Does Miss Barnfield still make your gowns, Anne?"

"Her eyesight is failing. Mama and I usually make our own now."

"Oh, my dear—such a bore for you! There is nothing so tedious as stitching. I have an ingenious French modiste. An artist—really, she is an artist. She is making me up an exquisite white gown for a do Bertie and I are going to at Carlton House next week. White crepe, with seed pearls all down the front. I look a regular dasher in it, I promise you."

"Annie likes white crepe," Robin said with a mischievous smile at his cousin.

"It would suit you better than the yellow you wore last night," Rosalie said. "That blue you're wearing is pretty, Anne. Is it new?"

"I've had it a few years," Anne admitted.

"Very nice color. The cut, of course, is not quite à la mode, but the color suits you."

Alex, sitting with Exmore and waiting for some masculine talk to get started between them, was listening to this conversation.

Soon Rosalie tired of examining the furnishings and

gowns. "I don't know how you all endure the tediousness of living in the country from head to toe of the year. Nothing ever seems to happen here."

"Nothing happen?" Mrs. Wickfield exclaimed, astonished. "Why, we've had a half dozen births in as many months here in the neighborhood, to say nothing of old Albert Secours dying and leaving no will. A fine brouhaha that was! Why, exciting things are happening every day. You only have to know where to look."

"And what to consider exciting," Alex added, tossing a mischievous smile to Anne.

She smiled back, but wanly. All her happy joking about her impoverished condition had deserted her during Rosalie's tirade. She looked wistfully at her visitor's elegant lutestring gown, at her white hands, which never did anything more strenuous than lift a teacup, at her dainty slippers, which would be cast aside long before they ever required mending.

As he watched, Alex's heart ached for her. Would he ever be able to give her all the fine things she deserved? Being deeply in love, he thought better beaux would fall into her lap, given half a chance. Perhaps he was being unfair to dangle after her.

Exmore soon began asking him questions about the Peninsular Campaign, which prevented Alex from overhearing the ladies' discussion, but he noticed that as Rosalie rattled merrily on, Anne's spirits sank lower, till in the end she was replying in monosyllables. After half an hour, she rose, saying, "I'll round up the children for tea. They'll need washing after their activities."

Alex followed her to the front door. "Has Rosalie been trying to smarten you up?"

She gave him a startled, conscious look. "What do you mean?"

"I'm speaking sartorially—is she telling you all the new fashions in London?"

"Yes, and making me realize what a dowd I am in the bargain."

"You don't look dowdy to me, Duck." He smiled. It wrenched her heart to see him being so brave, trying to cheer her, from the depths of his own problems.

"To her I do, but that's not why I'm peevish. How will you repay Exmore, Alex?"

"I don't know. I'll think about that tomorrow."

"It seems to me they don't need the money so badly. The things Rosalie has told us about buying in the past half hour must come to more than what you owe them. She's a part of the Penholme family, too. She should take the loss of her loan to Charlie and not pester you with it now."

"It was Exmore's money, not hers. He must be paid."

They called the children, and soon the whole throng was seated around the table. It was not the happy sort of meal recently enjoyed at Penholme. Rosalie chided her sisters for their lack of manners, and when Bung began talking about the frog he had caught at the pond, she scolded him for discussing such things at table.

"People eat them," he pointed out.

"The *French* eat them," she corrected.

"The French are people. What's wrong with talking about them at the table? It's no different from chickens or cows. We eat dead animals."

Rosalie pushed away her plate with a pained expression. "Till these ruffians have been taught some manners, Alex, you ought not to allow them into company. I don't approve of having children at table with adults. They invariably say something disgusting and usually make such a revolting mess of their food besides, that no one with any sensitivity can bear to eat a bite."

The less sensitive members finished their tea—even Rosalie had soon attacked her food again—but the party was not a great success. Everyone was relieved when the duchess entered her black carriage with the strawberry leaves on the door panels and was driven to Penholme, where she was soon complaining of the holes in the wall of the armaments room and the dust under her bed, in spite of dozens of servants. Alex quietly locked the door of the blue suite, to prevent her from seeing the charred curtains there.

The next diversion in the lives of the Penholmes and the Wickfields would be less unappealing to her grace. The children who had so marred the last outing would not be attending the spring assembly in Eastleigh, nor the dinner at Penholme before it, to which the Wickfields were invited.

Anne, weary of her rose and old yellow gowns, reached farther back into her closet to see what she could do with a blue moire gown of yore. She would look a quiz beside the elegant duchess and the merchants' daughters, but at least she would be in the company of the most elevated persons at the assembly, and she took what consolation she could from that. Rosalie did not spurn country do's. Having been raised at Penholme, she enjoyed to go again among her old friends and amaze them with her duke and her London style. As the Duchess of Exmore, with Bertie a notch above Penholme in precedence, she would get to open the dancing. She planned to flirt discreetly with her old beaux and break a dozen hearts before the night was over. She was in good spirits and, of more importance to her, in good looks.

Decked out in diamonds and silk, Rosalie did the family credit; Alex smiled to see her open the assembly. "She puts them all in the shade, doesn't she?" he asked Anne while they stood waiting to join in the dance.

"Yes," Anne said briefly, but added not a word of praise on the loveliest creature ever to have come out of the county.

The duchess was the undisputed queen of the party, but the king was not so easily ascertained. There was Bertie, the only duke present, to be considered, and there was Penholme, a returned officer and the local lord, but both of these gentlemen were run very hard by Lord Robin. He looked licked to a splinter in Charlie's black evening outfit by Weston. Rosalie was undecided whether to honor him or Penholme for the second dance, but in the end precedence won out, and she stood up with Alex. Her mind was more than half full of the impression she was making, but she saved a corner of it to look around for eligible ladies for her brothers. Before long, she had singled out a pair who were second only to her in fashion. Alex was unable to enlighten her as to their identity, but during the third dance, Robin told her they were the Anglin girls, Maggie and Marilla.

"Anglin? What kind of a name is that? I never heard of any Anglins hereabouts."

"They're new. Their papa is lately retired from London."

"I don't recognize the name from London society either. Who are they? They look unexceptionable."

"They're cits, Rosie," Robin said bluntly. "You wouldn't have heard of them, but I daresay you've heard of the Albion string of stores. They have a couple of them in London and one in Bath and Brighton—all over the place. Anglin is the owner."

It was a hard circumstance to a Penholme-Exmore, very much aware of her family bloodlines, that such rich girls should be so low-born. In appearance, however, they might pass for fine ladies, and as ladies Penholme and Robin they might also get by without their ancestors passing under too close a scrutiny. She was not so impetuous as to hand her brothers over without hearing what sort of accent came out of the girls' mouths and seeing whether they handled their cutlery at dinner with propriety. It was necessary that she see them at close range to determine whether they could conceal their origins, and for this, she must have them presented to her. Robin was not loath to perform the introduction; indeed, he performed with suspicious alacrity in the matter.

The girls were examined with the thoroughness of a horse breeder about to purchase a brood mare. It was not chest and eye and ankle that were studied but the presence (or absence) of pronounced aitches, the tilt of the head, whether lofty or hung low in high company. They gained a point immediately by holding their heads at the proper angle and blushing prettily as they expressed their delight in the presentation. Their features were seen to be pleasing, not outstanding enough to rival Rosalie's own, but with no raw-boned, common look about them. Rather fine-featured, actually. Both were a little inclined to tallness, but they carried themselves well and were a few inches short of being termed "ladders." The elder was the prettier, with brown eyes and hair and a good set of teeth. Miss Maggie was not unlike her, but the face was shorter, with a smattering of freckles that bespoke an unladylike familiarity with the sun. They were well-spoken, a matter of paramount importance; and of nearly equal merit, they were not in the least forthcoming. They realized very well the degree of condescension bestowed on them, and were suitably reverent.

Rosalie was a trifle vexed when Robin asked the younger to stand up with him, till it darted into her head that this was exactly as things ought to be. Miss Anglin, the elder

118

and slightly more desirable, must be left for Alex. Ignoring the fact that Alex had already found himself an heiress, she delivered a blushing Miss Anglin to his side to stand up with.

There was no longer any vestige of a doubt in her mind that Alex, the gudgeon, had settled on Anne Wickfield. Annie, the sly thing, was feigning a *tendre* after having chased Charlie for years as hard as her legs would carry her. She did not by any means despise Anne for this cleverness. She would have done exactly the same thing herself in Anne's place, if Alex's pockets were not so badly to let. It was pointless to think she could get Alex to London to make a truly brilliant match; he had never been a city buck. No, he would choose his bride from among the second-rate girls at this assembly, and of those present, Miss Anglin bore the crown.

Alex was not a high stickler. It was his intention to dance with anyone presented to him, and in particular he had intended to seek out the Anglin girls, as Robin referred to Maggie more often than mere chance would indicate. He was clearly interested in the girl, and, therefore, his elder brother intended to size her up. He was slightly less interested in this elder sister he was with, but as a future connection, she, too, was to be examined. He could find no glaring fault in her. She was a little shy, but he wasn't the sort of gentleman who enjoyed idle flirtation, so he approved of her quiet manners.

At the dance's end, he went along to where Robin and Miss Maggie stood. After he was presented to Maggie, he and Robin exchanged partners for the next set.

Rosalie darted over to join Anne, who had been standing up with Exmore. "Those are the Anglin girls," she told her spouse. "Their papa is Albion."

Exmore frowned. "I never heard of Lord Albion," he said.

"Not Lord Albion, love, he is a cit," she said, and laughed merrily. "Rich as Croesus, and he has no sons, just these two girls to inherit it all. He's retired, Robin tells me, which dilutes the aroma of trade. I think we have got Alex's problem solved. These two will make very fine brides, don't you think?"

"Penholme won't marry a merchant's daughter," Exmore objected at once.

"Pooh! At this point Alex would marry an actress if the dibs were in tune. He hasn't much choice, poor soul. I have met the girls and given them my approval. Don't you find them quite genteel, Anne?"

"They are well enough," Anne said coolly. Her glance strayed across the room to where Robin and Alex were conversing with the sisters. She was painfully aware that Miss Anglin was younger and much better outfitted than she was herself. Any stranger entering the room would take Miss Anglin for the fine lady.

Rosalie turned aside for a private word with Anne. "Alex *must* marry money, Anne," she said bluntly. "Don't let him waste your time playing up to you, for nothing can come of it. You must get busy and find yourself another parti. Now, who is that gentleman over there with his quizzing glass raised?" she asked. "I declare, it's Georgie Hamilton. I haven't seen him in a dog's age. Not a bad catch for you," she advised Anne. She raised her hand and waved him to her. This scion of a good county family, one of Rosalie's old court, came forward promptly, hoping for the distinction of a dance with the duchess, who did no more than say good evening before she put her white fingers on her duke's arm and led him off for a glass of wine.

Mr. Hamilton showed no aversion to standing up with

Miss Wickfield, nor she with him. She had already had a dance with Alex and knew perfectly well she would not have another till after the intermission, if he chose to honor her with two dances. Naturally, he must dance with other ladies, but when he went from one Anglin sister to the other, then at the end of that dance went to meet their parents, she began to fear Rosalie's advice was being heeded.

When Alex sat the next dance out with the parents, she was definitely miffed, and when the Exmores darted up to join them, she was furious. It looked as if Rosalie was having her way—as usual. Of course, it was only the money she was after, and in the usual frank way of the Penholmes, she didn't bother to conceal it. Alex needed money, certainly, but it was only a temporary shortage. Even the extra debt to Exmore didn't positively eclipse him. How could he smile so dotingly on Miss Anglin when it was her he loved? She had been drawing near to this conclusion for several days and was convinced she was right. Every word he said, every look and gesture, proclaimed it, but since the moment he had been presented to Miss Anglin, he hadn't once looked in her direction.

She almost began to think he had suffered a change of heart. His interest in her had been equally sudden, when she took time to think about it. He hadn't used to care for her, but then, on the day he had come home, he had begun dangling after her most markedly. He hadn't actually seen any other girls since he had come. This was the first time he had gone into public society, and at his first exposure to other girls, he'd forgotten her. He had been lonesome in Spain and latched on to the first English lady he came across; that was all it was. What a fool she had been to think it meant anything. Really, she hardly knew Alex. He was another Charles in the petticoat line and would likely end up chasing all the girls, now that he was out in public. Yes, there had been an air of his being very much aware of his own attractiveness, as she considered it.

He finally tore himself away from the Anglins and danced with some of his old friends, the rector's daughters and others, but when it was time for dinner, he came back to Mrs. Wickfield and Anne.

"Rosie is picking out a table large enough for us all," he said, offering each lady an arm. Anne was hurt and angry, but she was too proud to allow it to show. The cunning Rosalie had found a table large enough for not only their party but the entire Anglin ménage as well.

"How nice," Anne said brightly.

She pretended not to notice when Alex drew Mrs. Anglin's chair. Robin did the pretty for her, whispering in her ear, "Be prepared to duck the splash of dunking biscuits."

Mrs. Anglin did not dunk her biscuits, for no biscuits were served. She did not eat her peas with her knife or her chicken with her fingers or do any other uncivilized thing. Till the dessert was served, she did nothing to disgrace herself, unless some high sticklers might consider a nearly total silence a disgrace. It's true she took up a spoon rather than a fork for dessert, but as soon as she saw the duchess pick up a fork, she quietly changed her spoon for the proper utensil.

Mr. Anglin, who preferred to be called Albion, was a loud, clamoring man with a voice that could be heard a county away. He was red of complexion, gray-haired, and looked extremely uncomfortable in his tight-fitting jacket and cravat, though both were of the finest workmanship. Rosalie saw he was one of those men no tailor could do anything with. Weston himself couldn't make a gentleman of this cit. She could not like his bragging about being a shopkeeper, and while she adored that he was good for a million pounds if sold out on the spot, she could not admire his saying it so publicly, so loud, and so often. It was clearly his way of calculating a man's true worth, to put him up on the auction block with all his worldly goods and chattels and see just what price he would fetch under the hammer.

"What do you figure Altmire's worth?" he asked Alex. He had singled out Penholme as his special confidant. "If Ronleigh Hall and all the heirlooms and artworks and the rest of it were put on the block, would he fetch a million, do you figure?"

"I confess I have no idea," Alex answered.

"Do you know what I figure he's worth? Seventy-five thousand pounds. That's what. I did a little calculating . . ." He went on to advise Alex how he had made a swift assessment of furnishings and acres on his one visit to Ronleigh Hall and come up with the sum of seventy-five thousand pounds. "Not guineas, mind—pounds! And that's assuming he has no mortgage, which I couldn't find out," he added scrupulously. "It's odd, don't ye think, that a man of so little goods is tooted up as a nabob?"

"The Altmires have always had a deal of influence in the political field," Alex explained, but the cabinet members, the positions at court, the directorship of several large companies—all were wiped away by a sweep of Albion's arm.

"Seventy-five thousand pounds. That's what he could come up with if he sold everything he owns. I could buy him up and never feel the pinch."

Alex sat waiting for an assessment of himself if sold up, and disliked having to confess to mortgages. But no confession was necessary. Albion knew it all. "I hear that brother of yours got you into deep water before he passed on," he said in a loud voice.

"We are experiencing a temporary difficulty," Alex admitted with foreboding of more minute revelations to come.

"He was an expensive fellow. What he took out on Penholme must bring your mortgage to something in the neighborhood of forty thousand," he ventured with a brightly questioning eye.

"Something like that," Alex admitted.

"Of course, you've got the other little place I've heard Lord Robin mention—Sawburne, I think it's called."

"Yes, with five hundred acres. That is Robin's inheritance, however."

"That's wise of you." Albion congratulated him with such an approving nod that Alex had to wonder what he meant. He wasn't left long in doubt. "The thing is, as ye obviously know very well, the agents will move slow in taking Penholme away from you. Only a small market for them big places, whereas any number of folks would be after a tidy little property like Sawburne. Then, too, they hesitate to move against a noble family property. If push came to shove, what would be done is they'd sell Sawburne on you and take the revenue to pay the interest on the Penholme mortgage. With Sawburne safe in Lord Robin's name, they must take Penholme or nothing. They'll think a long while before they pull a stunt like that on a veteran. You got something for those three years spent in Spain."

"We're not in quite such deep waters as that," Alex assured him. "I'd sell the London place before I'd let them take Penholme."

"By the time you'd paid off the London mortgage, though, there'd not be much left."

"The London house is not mortgaged," Alex said, pokering up at such detailed and public inquisition.

"Is that so? Is that so, indeed? I heard otherwise." An extremely disbelieving eye narrowed on Penholme.

Alex looked at him in alarm. "May I ask where you heard it, sir?"

"In the city. I have many contacts there. Of course, they're not your set and were very likely out in their news. Naturally you know whether the London house is mortgaged."

"It isn't," Alex said firmly, but was soon besieged by a doubt. There had never been a mortgage on the London house. Surely Charles hadn't put one on it, as well as Penholme and Sawburne and selling the hunting box outright and the loan from Exmore. No one, not even Charlie, could have gone through such a mountain of money as that. He shook away the nagging worry and listened to Albion.

"What kind of a place is Spain? Any money to be made at all?"

"I spent my time in the mountains and bogs. I wasn't thinking about making money but saving my skin," Alex said.

"I see no possibilities for Spain," Albion admitted sadly. "Their leather is good, but with the supply cut off since the war, folks have gotten out of the way of demanding Spanish leather. And after the war, the metal in demand will be iron for plowshares, not fine steel for swords. Italy, now—there's the olive oil trade, and some halfway decent dry goods. I did a tidy bit of trade with Italy."

The next victim for Albion's financial scrutiny was Exmore, who had to endure having his possessions shouted across the table. The meal was some strange combination of comedy and farce, with Albion clearly the leading character. His companions were by turn embarrassed by him and for him, but he had no notion he was doing anything but showing a polite interest. The matter of paramount importance in his world was money; he rarely discussed anything else, and he was as eager to present his own financial statement as to hear anyone else's.

He meant to see his daughters marry above themselves—

a title, if possible—and he was willing to pay out a reasonable sum for the privilege. It was as well as settled in his own mind that he would have to redeem Sawburne and eventually add a few thousand acres to it. Five thousand, he figured for a wedding gift to the couple, with, say, twenty-five thousand for Maggie's dowry. He had as yet no accurate idea what the title of countess was worth on the market, but he would look into it—scan the recent transactions in London and see what Rogers had paid for his daughter's title. He didn't intend to be rooked, but on the other hand, he was not a skint. He'd make a fair barter.

Of all the noble crowd, it was Rosalie he liked best. Her husband was a stiff-rumped dullard, and Penholme, too, a bit high in the instep, but Rosalie was what he'd call a real lady. The saucy minx even got him to stand up with her for a country dance—jigging was a thing he didn't do in the usual way—but she had such a cute manner about her that he was beguiled into it. Even if she hadn't been a duchess, he would have done it. When she called him Albion and smiled at him, he half felt he was Lord Albion, and his old chest swelled. Her hints that Penholme was attracted to Marilla went down exceedingly well, and when she batted her long lashes at him and said of course poor Penholme was dreadfully in trouble and wouldn't bring too tidy a sum if sold up, he said merrily that there was no problem in that, begad, no problem at all.

Alex asked Anne to stand up for another dance after dinner. She accepted, but with little enthusiasm. Alex observed her stiff face and tried to talk her back into spirits.

"You're peeved to see us making such a fuss over the Anglins," he said.

"Not in the least. I am only relieved Albion didn't put Mama and me on the block. We would have blushed to admit our combined resources are not more than five

126

hundred per annum—the sum Maggie gets for pin money, as we all know now. Since the way out of one's fiscal difficulties is to marry a merchant, I am sorry Mr. Anglin has no sons."

"I know you don't like to see such blood come into the family, but there's a time for everything, and this is *not* the time to pull pedigree. We have to come down off our high ropes and do what we can to redeem our former glory. Rosalie is right, you know."

"Who am I to contradict a duchess?"

"Old Anglin is not overly refined, but the girls are quite nice, don't you think?"

It angered her that she could find no real fault in them. "Which one is it you fancy, Alex?" she asked.

"The question is which does Rob fancy, and it is, of course, the younger, Maggie. I prefer the elder myself."

"That is convenient, then—it won't be necessary for you and Robin to draw straws."

"It wouldn't do for me to dangle after Rob's woman, would it? Though I must say, he seems a little more attracted to mine than I can quite like."

Anne took a quick breath and stiffened. "I never noticed it. I don't think he cares for her overly much," she said with a glance around the room for Miss Anglin. Sure enough, there was Robin capering at her heels. But it was usually Maggie that Robin spoke of.

"*I* have noticed it. Unless I make a beeline to her chair, he beats me to her every time. And since he's become so stylish in Charlie's outfits, there's no denying he cuts a good figure. Annie, we can't talk here. Let's sit this dance out." He walked from the floor, holding her arm in a tight grip.

An angry spark lit her eye. "You'll have to trim him into line, Major."

Alex's jaw firmed, and when he reached the edge of the

room, he kept walking to the door. He opened it and they went out into the cool night. This was considered rather racy behavior, but Anne was old enough and Alex high enough that it was saved from being called fast.

"I have more than one rebel to trim into line. What are *you* so angry about? I seem to have missed a beat here."

"You were never so on the mark as Charles and Robin," she snipped.

An angry flush rose from his collar, and his voice when he answered was thin. "I never hoped to compete with Charles, certainly, but I didn't look to Robin for competition."

"Then you shouldn't have been egging him on to admire the Anglins so assiduously, ever since your return. It's you who put this idea of marrying an Anglin in his head. He never mentioned it till you came back, expressing concern that he not dangle after an 'ineligible lady.' Between you and Rosalie, you're as good as pushing him to the altar."

Alex gave a frown of confusion. "An eligible lady would be the best thing for him—for us both, and you must know it as well as anyone. How else is he to make a go of Sawburne?"

She heard that unthinking "us both" and was turned to stone, which soon heated to lava. "Is that why you are in such an almighty rush to give it to him? So he'll be hobbled with the mortgage and *have* to marry her?"

Alex stared in disbelief. "You make me sound like a conniving monster! I'm giving it to him because I know how it feels to be robbed by your own brother. Yes, I dare to utter the bald truth about Charles. If any of us are forced into irregular matches, it is Charles who is to blame, not I. I didn't mortgage Robin's inheritance. But I know you won't say a word against Charles, so you'll just have to smile and bear it that a Penholme marries a cit's daughter."

"An officer and a gentleman should have the gumption to take responsibility for his own life. Very few men are born with silver spoons in their mouths. They don't all use it as an excuse to make a profitable marriage of convenience."

"I take full responsibility for my own life, not Robin's. *I'm* not the one planning to marry an Anglin. Though Robin is, I trust, a gentleman, you forget he was never an officer. I don't know what had been between the two of you before my return. Of course, he bears a strong superficial resemblance to Charles, and that must always attract you, eh, Anne? I happened not to be born with a hero's face and physique, but by God I'd rather be my ugly self than a beautiful sham."

"Robin is not a sham!"

"I wasn't talking about Robin, then. Of course it's Robin who trails your skirts these days. Always running to you the minute he's bolted his wine. Unless I make a dash to your side, he's there before me, but I truly don't believe it to be love on his part."

Realization dawned on Anne that a misunderstanding had gotten loose between them. He thought she was romantically interested in Robin, and she had mistakenly supposed his reference to "my woman" meant Miss Anglin. When the truth tumbled into place, she felt foolish and elated and sorry all at the same time. She was especially sorry she had thrown Charles in his face, for that was what she had done in her fit of jealousy.

She swallowed convulsively and tried to find a graceful way out of the mess. "You said 'us both'—I mean, about marrying the Anglin girls."

Alex's stiff shoulders relaxed; a slow smile crept across his face. "Annie," he said, his words a caress, "is that what had you in a pelter? I am greatly flattered." He drew her into his arms slowly, gazing at her face all the while as she gazed back silently. He pulled her head to his shoulder and held it there, gently patting it.

"Oh, Alex, you are a goose!" she said. Her voice trembled with emotion. "Robin is like a young brother to me."

He tilted her chin up to him, and they stood in the moonlight. She felt as if they were alone in some beautifully forgotten corner of the universe. The old familiar hawthorne bushes that edged the yard of the assembly hall provided concealment from the street, and behind them the curtained windows cut them off from the dancers. Her blood quickened as Alex gazed at her. Then his head descended slowly, irrevocably, to hers, obliterating the moon and the view and worldly cares. She was crushed against him, his lips bruising hers with a hungry, devouring kiss that was unlike gentle Alex in its ruthlessness. Her response was alien to her as well. She felt a wild and heady excitement, a flame licking through her veins, heating her vitals, and urging her on to some unknown madness.

When he finally stopped, she could only stare at him in wonder. "You'll never know how long I've imagined this, Annie," he said in a husky voice.

"I never . . ." She stopped and shook her head in confusion. She had never imagined, never dreamed of, such a thing.

"I know," he said. "I imagined enough for us both. Is our argument over?"

"Yes, all over."

"Good. Who won?"

"I did; I had the advantage of knowing what we were arguing about, you see," she said, and withdrew from him. They strolled arm in arm along the covered walk, talking. She was acutely aware of the new intimacy between them, sensed it in Alex's more revealing manner.

"We both won. You deserve a handicap, being pitched

130

against a professional soldier like me. The very worst soldier there ever was, too. I hated pulling the trigger. I let dozens of Frenchies escape when I could have plugged them in the back. I daresay I'd be court-martialed if Hookey ever found out how I carried on. I couldn't help thinking that like me, they had families and a girl or a wife back home and probably wished they had never seen the shores of Spain.''

"You're too kindhearted to be a soldier. I don't know whatever possessed you to enlist."

"Don't you, Annie? I thought you were beginning to understand why."

"Robin told me about the fights with Charles. I think it was awful, the way he plundered Penholme."

"I'm demmed sorry I let myself be driven out, but who would have dreamed Charlie would die so young? Anglin's knock about the London mortgage has me worried. You don't suppose Charlie mortgaged *it* on us, too, do you? I can't believe it."

"How would Anglin know?"

"He knew about the second mortgage on Penholme— the exact amount."

"He doesn't know whether Ronleigh Hall is mortgaged."

"Still, I must go back to London with Rosie and Exmore and find how things stand there. If Charlie didn't mortgage it, I must do it myself. We won't need it for a few years, till Loo is ready to make her bows. You don't care about going to London for the Season, do you?"

"I never miss a Season!" she joked, for, of course, Alex knew she had never had one in her life, and it was as clear as crystal that he intended to marry her, even if he hadn't said so.

They soon reentered the hall. The assembly became suddenly very enjoyable to Miss Wickfield. She regretted when it was over. She and her mother were taken home in Alex's carriage, and at some point during the evening he had settled on going to London with the Exmores the next morning and staying with them for a few days. They would all stop at Rosedale on their way to see if the ladies had any commissions for him.

"White crepe or anything of that sort," he added with a secret smile.

"Going to pawn your gold toothpick, Alex?" she asked. "You know I have no money."

"The mystery of the gold spear is solved. Rosie says it's part of a game—fiddlesticks, I think. A gilt stick is a feature of importance. All the crack to have a real gold stick, so she pocketed it. She wanted a memento of Charles."

Anne thought it was rather a solid gold stick Rosie wanted but was in too good a humor to say so. "I see."

"I offered it to you first, and you didn't know enough to grab it," he reminded her.

"I didn't particularly want a memento of Charles."

"I noticed," he said, and applied a light pressure to her fingers as he left the ladies at the door.

Now, is that what he was up to? Anne wondered. She began to think Alex was more devious than she had ever suspected. He had been testing her, and without even knowing it, she had passed—because she had stopped caring for Charles ages ago. Her only feeling for him now was one of deep disgust.

Chapter Eleven

When Alex had his carriage stopped at Rosedale on his way to London next morning, Rosalie did likewise, leaving her husband alone while she took her leave of the Wickfields.

"Was it not a famous party last night?" She laughed, in a gay mood to be returning to her beloved London. "I had two country dances with Albion, and my arm is sore this morning. He nearly wrenched it from the socket going down the line. I like him excessively, much better than if he tried to be genteel, like his wife. What a blight the woman is, to be sure. *He* is a splendid barbarian, but that wife—my, has she a tongue, do you think? I didn't hear her say boo to a goose the whole night long. But she will come along. She dropped her spoon and took up her fork as soon as ever I raise an eyebrow at her. The girls are quite unexceptionable. I shan't blush to present them. We shall cover up Miss Maggie's bran face with rice powder—poor creature, her freckles positively glow. The other will do as she is, after I have my coiffeur take her crimped locks in hand."

"Is there anything we can do for you in London?" Alex asked when he could edge in a word.

Before the ladies had time to answer, Rosalie spoke again. "I'll send you a brochure on the Carlton House tables, Aunt Alice. I still have it somewhere around the house. It will look very good just there, where I told you. And in the meanwhile you may as well have the paper hangers in, for you will not be happy with these dim walls."

"Don't worry if you can't find it," Mrs. Wickfield answered.

"I shan't forget you either, Annie," the duchess promised.

"I can't think of a single thing I want. Very likely something will come to me as soon as the carriage leaves the door."

"Widgeon!" Rosalie laughed. "I mean your beau. Now that we have Robin and Alex settled up with the Anglin *soeurs*, I shall have all my mind free to find a parti for you. It cannot be impossible," she added in a voice that suggested it would be a daunting task all the same. Her bright eyes flashed from Anne to Alex as she spoke. "I have the cleverest idea," she rattled on as she saw the two exchange a secret smile that was so much more convincing than mere words. "We shall stop at the Anglins' palace *en passant* and see just how vulgarly overdone it is. Crystal chandeliers all over, red velvet drapes, and spanking-new everything, I make no doubt."

"I haven't heard Albion has his place open to tours," Alex said ironically.

"Another goose!" Rosalie exclaimed. "I shall ask them if you can perform any little commission for them in the city, and then you will have a chance to stop again on your way home and make eyes at Miss Anglin."

"Officious, sis. Albion goes up to London at least once a week. He was telling me so just last night."

"Still, he will not take it amiss that Lord Penholme honors him with the offer," she pointed out. "He'll be flattered to death."

Alex just shook his head. "We'd best be getting on," he suggested. "Exmore is waiting in the carriage."

"Lud, you don't have to worry about him. He will be sound asleep by now," Rosalie said. But she was eager to leave and got up from her seat.

The Wickfields walked to the carriages with their guests to exchange half a dozen good-byes before returning to the saloon with that little feeling of letdown that always remains behind when one sees others off on a trip.

London was some seventy miles away. With the delay of stopping at Anglins', where Albion was sharp enough to find a commission to ensure Penholme's return, it was late evening when the carriages pulled up to the door of Exmore's mansion on Belgrave Square. The duchess's first thought was to look over her invitations; her second was to run up to her children, as it was too late to have them brought down. She *did* love them, the more so as they had both had the wits to have been born boys and secure the family title.

The first feature of the house that took Alex's attention was the gas light. It gave off such unaccustomed brightness that it seemed impossible night had fallen outdoors. He had never seen gas light before. It had just been coming into vogue when he had left three years ago, and this was the first home he had visited that used it. His amazement pleased both his sister and Exmore very well. They took him from lamp to lamp, turning the adjustment knob higher and lower to show him how it was capable of giving as much or as little illumination as was wanted. Exmore extinguished one lamp to demonstrate how it was lit, a procedure that caused not only Alex but also Rosalie to take a long step backward, though the jet of flame that leaped out was not so dangerous as he had supposed it must be.

"It gives a dandy light, but still, I think it must be very dangerous," Alex decreed. "And there are pipes under the ground to deliver the gas, you say? We'll be fortunate if half of London isn't blown sky-high with it."

"They've been using it in factories for a few years now with no trouble," Exmore assured him. "It's actually safer than conventional lighting. The war has cut down the supply of whale oil and Russian tallow, thus raising the price. Insurance rates are cheaper with gas, too. It is the coming thing—mark my words. They have it lighting the streets of St. Margaret's Parish in Westminster—it attracts a crowd each night to see it. Why, there are over twenty miles of gas mains in London already. The day isn't long off when the entire city will be using it."

"Is it a government-run thing?" Alex inquired. "I'm completely out of it, from having been abroad so long."

"It was inaugurated before you left," Exmore pointed out. "It is a private business with a charter from the government. The Gas, Light and Coke Company, it is called. It started in 1812. I'm surprised Charles didn't mention it to you. He took an interest from the start. A bunch of sharp businessmen got it up, with bankers and some noble patrons to finance it. It was a German fellow got it all started—Albrect Winzer was his name—but he's anglicized it to Albert Winsor now."

"We got these sweet little fixtures to go with it," Rosalie told her brother, and took him from one metal bracket to another, each with its own glass globe to magnify the light and protect the surroundings from the direct flame "It cost a fortune, which is why we would like to get the money you owe us," she added in a low aside beyond her husband's hearing. Such a plethora of excuses had been

136

put forward for needing the money that Alex scarcely listened.

The Exmores had no social engagements that evening, so the time was passed *en famille,* with an early retirement to recover from the weariness of travel. In the morning, Rosalie was much of a mind to send her brother off to her husband's tailor to outfit him in a higher style before parading him before her friends, but Alex told her that was not his intention. As already stated, he had come on business, and without even the pleasure of a strut down Bond Street on his arm, she had to let him go.

His first stop was the handsome red-brick family home on Berkeley Square. He was loath to enter it when he saw the knocker off and the shutters closed. He stepped into a house nearly black, leaving the front door ajar till he got the lamps lit. Exmore had mentioned Charlie's interest in the new gas light, but his interest had not extended to having it installed in his own home. Alex lit several candles and stood in the airless room looking about for ghosts of Charles. He half feared his brother would have ransacked the place, sold off plate and pictures, but his spending had not reached quite that pitch.

Things were intact, as far as Alex could tell. He had actually spent very little time in London. He made a cursory inspection of the family quarters, then returned to the study, where business papers were usually kept. The desk and drawers were empty—not so much as a bank statement or a bill. The family's man of business would have been here before him, of course. Alex locked the house and went straight to the office of Snelgrove and Snelgrove, where no Snelgrove had worked for one hundred years, the firm having been taken over by in-laws named Naismith.

Mr. Naismith the elder was a gaunt man with straight white hair pulled severely across his scalp. He ushered

Penholme into his office with a welcoming smile that reminded Alex of the rictus he had seen on dead soldiers in Spain. Alex had never had occasion to meet the man before, but Naismith had served both his father and Charles, so was acquainted with all the family business affairs. Penholme was made to feel at home with a glass of sherry and a cheroot cigar, treats saved for noble clients.

"I was happy to learn you are safely returned to us, milord," Mr. Naismith began, lending a social air to the occasion by a reference to matters in the Peninsula. This was not why Alex had come, and he reverted directly to business. Though the firm handled only London matters of finance, Naismith knew enough of the general situation that he inquired discreetly as to whether Penholme would be able to set the Hall to rights.

"I hope so. We're heavily mortgaged," Alex admitted. "There is the London house to fall back on, however. I may find it necessary to take out a small mortgage on it."

Naismith's pale eyes blinked. "Ah, another mortgage . . ."

Alex's heart plunged. "Another mortgage?" he asked in a sepulchral tone.

"There is the mortgage for eight thousand the late earl took out some months before his death. The place is worth more—ten thousand, I should think—but eighty percent is already a heavy mortgage, the heaviest your brother could raise at the time."

Once, at Badajos, Alex had found himself cut off from his army, caught behind the enemy line with only his batman, the two of them surrounded by enemies. He had thought he would die that night. He could hear not a dozen feet away from him French soldiers talking. He knew the taste of fear, of panic, and he tasted it now at the back of his throat. It was a sharp, dry sensation, accompanied by a heightened awareness of irrelevant details around him. In Spain that night, he had noticed how brightly the stars shone, had been minutely aware of a sharp stone digging into his leg as he sat cramped and silent.

Now he looked at a bad picture of Anne Hathaway's cottage, and knew he would remember for the rest of his life the exact lineaments of it. The three chimneys, the left part of the house higher than the right, the thatched roof. At Badajos, he and Lehman had escaped by crawling on their bellies like snakes, inching forward an inch at a time, fearing every rustle of the grass, just waiting to be discovered and killed. He saw no means of exit this time. He was surrounded by debts, and the money he had been counting on was gone. Another eight thousand pounds poured down the bottomless pit of Charles's senseless spending. What had ailed him, that he could waste the family money so wantonly? Lowering his eyes from the picture on the wall, Alex saw Mr. Naismith regarding him with a commiserating eye.

"It cannot be impossible to raise a small sum," Naismith suggested hopefully. "How much do you urgently require? You mentioned a small mortgage."

Alex was reluctant to go into all the disagreeable, impossible details till he had time to think. "I'll look over my accounts and let you know."

"These bills waiting for payment," Naismith went on, pulling out a great folder stuffed with unpaid bills, "can wait. Tradesmen, for the most part. I paid off your brother's gambling debts from the bequest the estate came into from your uncle Cyrus Fender last year. I knew you would wish to have them taken care of as soon as possible. I also kept up payments on the London mortgage."

Alex knew vaguely he had once had an uncle Cyrus Fender. He didn't know the man had died, and he had not thought the family would inherit anything from him. With an apathy born of despair, he inquired how much it had amounted to.

"Ten thousand pounds," Naismith said calmly.

Another fortune sown on the winds by his brother. His delightful, charming brother, whom all the world loved. Another ten thousand on top of the eight thousand mortgage on the house. There couldn't be another creature in the country who spent such sums, unless it should be the Prince of Wales, and he, at least, had the whole country to support him.

"What is the total of this batch of bills?" Alex asked, hefting the folder.

"It is nothing to worry about. Tailors and bootmakers and hatmakers. Few gentlemen presented such a fine appearance as the late Lord Penholme. A few bills from jewelers. Your brother was popular with the ladies," he ventured playfully.

"How much?" Alex repeated in a louder, harsher voice.

"I have it figured out here. Four thousand and five hundred, give or take a few guineas."

Nothing to worry about! A mere drop in the bottomless bucket of Charles's improvidence. "We'll let the merchants wait a little longer," Alex said, rising. He felt a hundred years old. His very joints protested at the effort of moving.

"Oh, they are not worried about getting their money. They were all happy for your brother's patronage. His appearance did them credit."

Not worried, but they should be. They weren't aware that Penholme was mortgaged to the tune of forty thousand, Sawburne to three, the Leicester property sold outright, that Charles had gotten the family into such debt that they'd be lucky to get a shilling on the pound when he was forced to declare himself a bankrupt.

"There are a few assets, what?" Naismith asked archly, but more than "a few" were needed. "A few investments." Alex gave a hopeful look. "The shipbuilding company was not profitable, alas. He lost a good sum on that, though it's still worth something—a few hundred. The wiser course would be to hang on till after the war, but you could sell them now . . ."

"A few hundred won't make much difference."

"Fortunately some of his other ventures did a little better. Would you like to take your brother's papers home with you? Look them over at your leisure, and we'll have a good meeting after you are in possession of the facts. Not much we can do till you have all the facts before you."

Naismith began pulling out folders and had them stuffed into a large box for Penholme to take to his carriage. A clerk was called to save his lordship the indignity of carrying a box.

"These are the stocks here," Naismith said, handing a slim folder to Alex. "A pity about the shipbuilding company. I thought it might prove profitable, but with the war disrupting shipping . . ."

"Yes, a pity," Alex said. He put the folder under his arm and left. He threw the material in a heap on one banquette of the carriage and directed the groom to take him to Hyde Park. He got out at Tyburn Turnpike House and walked along in a sort of daze. Tyburn, that old historical site of executions, suited his mood. He stopped at Tyburn tree, now replaced with an inscribed stone, and thought of Cromwell hanging there, and Jack Sheppard. He was at the end of a rope himself; he might as well be hanging there with all his troubles behind him. It hardly seemed worth surviving a war, to come home to this.

How bright the future had looked a few short weeks ago. In his eagerness to get home, he'd left with his wound still open, thinking it would heal during the voyage, only to have it become infected during the trip. But that was only a physical wound—one gritted one's teeth and endured the short agony of cauterization. How was this other hurt, this deep, creeping ache that must be despair, to be overcome? He thought of his family, the children raised with high expectations, who must be farmed out to obliging relatives, for it was beginning to look as though he might lose even Penholme. It wasn't fair to his tenants to make them go on living in damp, unhealthy cottages, working farms that needed money put into them to be profitable. Some smart, retired merchant like Anglin could afford to set Penholme back on its feet. He would lose it—the stain of failure would besmirch his name, not Charles's. And Annie—was he to lose her now, after so much waiting, and when she was within his grasp?

Annie . . . A sad smile settled on him as he remembered her mending her blue slippers and regretting the white crepe, but in good humor. "An officer and a gentleman should have more gumption!" she had told him. What good was gumption when unaccompanied by money? Sell the London house? He'd clear two thousand, a laughable sum, in the face of his debts. All he had was his title. A title ought to be worth something. . . . Any number of sine-cures might be open to a lord returned from the war in Spain. An ambassadorship or some government post would be provided. Prinny treated his officers with liberality.

He looked into the muddy waters of that misnamed lake the Serpentine, which was nearly a perfect parallelogram, and thought its creator, Queen Caroline, had been nearly as foolish as Charles to have spent a reputed twenty thousand pounds for the dirty, unappetizing little puddle. The world was full of fools and scoundrels—how did it come that they were invariably the ones who got their hands on money?

How much would a sinecure at court pay? Enough to hold on to Penholme, to meet the staggering mortgage? Perhaps, if one lived like a hermit for a couple of decades and could endure the guilt of making his tenants live in squalor. Was it fair to offer a lady a battle-torn body, scarred for life, and a crippling burden of debt? Possibly even a life of exile, if it turned out he was given an ambassadorship. Annie loved her roots and her home as much as he did himself.

Alive or dead, Charles was still between them. Dashing, daring, handsome, reckless Charles, who had infatuated Anne as he had all the other girls, and treated her as badly, too. Perhaps it was partly Alex's fault. He had felt he had no chance to win her while Charles was alive, and nothing to offer her. He had seen her only when he could find an excuse—a brace of partridge or a rabbit, which he was obliged to say came from Charles, the lord of the manor. And, of course, the family parties, when he had had the excruciating pain of seeing her smile at Charles and hardly glancing in his own direction. But with Charles dead, it looked as though all that was changing. He had always known they'd be pinched for money at first, but Annie wouldn't cavil at that.

His delight at learning she cared for him was short-lived. It had lasted exactly thirty-six hours; from eleven o'clock the night of the assembly till eleven this morning. The dream of having her at the Hall, a bride for himself and a mother for the children, had seemed possible for exactly thirty-six hours. At least he hadn't offered for her; he would not have the shame of withdrawing his offer. Yet he regretted that he had not. He could not honorably offer now, in his position, but had the wedding already been set, she wouldn't back down. She would face with him what he must now face alone. He wouldn't mind being exiled to Austria or some such place if only Annie could go with him.

He walked for two hours, not noticing when the carriages started to arrive, but the increased traffic began to annoy his solitude after a while, and he went to his carriage, to return to Exmore's. It was his family's custom to share all the news, however unpleasant, and talk it out thoroughly, but today he couldn't face it. Rosalie's eager face told him she expected to receive her money, possibly even that minute, and he had to make an excuse about that.

"I have some debts of Charles's that must be taken care of immediately," he explained. "Exmore said his need wasn't urgent. I'll pay him as soon as I can."

"It seems a pity to me that Harriet Wilson must take precedence over us, but there will be a great scandal if her jewelry isn't paid for. I suppose that is the debt you refer to."

"Who is Harriet Wilson?" Alex asked.

"Oh, Alex, really! Have you been living in Spain or on the moon? I made sure even *you* would know about the Wilson sisters. Why, Wellington himself is one of Harriet's beaux, you must know. Three prissy little whores who have every buck and beau in the city languishing after them. Charles was carrying on with Harriet before he died, and it was said he was the one who gave her that diamond necklace she wore to the opera. I think he might have paid Exmore instead! Of course, the Wilsons are very good ton," she added forgivingly.

Alex stared at her condoning tone. "How could you let him do it, Rosie? He's *ruined* this family. He hardly behaved like a rational man."

"He didn't seen very worried. In fact, after you left, he said you had read him a Bear Garden jaw, and he was going to make some solid investments."

"Yes, in a shipping company that's sunk."

"Even when he was dying, he didn't appear unduly concerned. I made a point to be with him at the end, you know," she said in a saintly voice. "I mentioned to him that he still owed Exmore and wondered if he had any suggestion as to how we might get our money."

Alex stared at this untimely dun, but Rosie was not disconcerted. "Well, I knew that once the will went into escrow, if that is the proper term, it would take eons to get our money, but Charles said not to worry."

"I don't believe he even knew what he owed. He'd run out of control completely. He hadn't sold off the furnishings; that's about all that remains. You are welcome to take your money in merchandise from the house if you like, before it is put up to auction."

"Oh, Alex, you're not going to have an auction! So vulgar. Why, you're worse than Charles."

"Yes, I have taken the cavalier notion to destroy the family's dignity and fortune, after Charles's careful guardianship, Rosalie. Better dip in and grab what is owed you, before the bailiffs move in."

"There is no need to be satirical. I knew how it would be once you took over," she snipped, and began assessing what value she could get away with putting on his possessions and what increase she might realize at a private sale later.

"Think about it. I'm returning to Penholme at once."

"What, going back already? You haven't seen Aunt Lucretia or ordered new jackets or anything."

"I'll write to Lucretia, and I won't be going anywhere that I need new jackets." His gait was dragging as he left

145

the room. Rosalie shook her head sadly. Alex had never had the spirit of Charles. Charles would only laugh at this contretemps and begin making eyes at the richest heiress in London.

"You'd best get home and begin making eyes at Miss Anglin, then," she said.

The duchess sent a footman to inquire as to whether her brother wanted the papers from his solicitor taken up, but as he was leaving so soon, he left them in the carriage. She did succeed in getting him to remain one night, as an early-morning start would prevent him from having to stay overnight at an inn. She urged him out to the theater with her and Exmore, but he elected to stay at home and spent his night tallying up long columns of figures, of which the assets always formed the smaller total. He left early the next morning, with Rosalie urging him to let her have her money as soon as possible. Anglin would not object to forwarding him a measly few thousand.

Alex realized this great compulsion to get back to Penholme was irrational, but like a wounded fox seeking its hole, he felt an instinctive desire to crawl home and lick his wounds, to staunch the flow of life-giving blood. He should stay in London, put the house up for sale, the furnishings at auction, start that breaking up of the family inheritance that must inevitably now occur. It broke his heart to do it. He must at least consider it in peace and quiet awhile, to see if there was any possible way to avoid such a drastic, calamitous step, and Naismith had not rushed him at all. The clever thing to do, of course, would be to court Miss Anglin, but he had never been one to put cleverness above right.

He knew he must retrace his steps within a few days, and the journey was uncomfortable with his shoulder still not completely healed, but he felt an atavistic need to be home, to see that the children were well, the place not burned down around their ears. But most of all, he wanted to see Anne. How could he tell her? What possible words could he find to soften the blow?

Chapter Twelve

Penholme's commission for Albion was no more than to bring him the most recent papers, and with Rosalie a willing ally in the plan, she parted with her own copies. Alex was in a deep study all the way home. He noticed neither the traffic, the pretty countryside, nor the jostling of the carriage. As they passed through Winchester, he realized they were getting close to home, and firmed up his plan to ingratiate himself with the Anglins, for Robin's sake. This was done by stepping in to take a glass of wine with them.

As his tired eyes looked around the luxurious house, he felt none of Rosalie's amusement at the appointments. Everything bright and new, and of the most expensive, if not always of the most refined taste.

Albion glanced at the papers brought and reached into his pocket to produce the payment. That would amuse Rosalie, too, but in his present mood, it impressed Penholme favorably. "I make it just two pence beneath a shilling. Don't worry about the change," he said.

"That's quite all right—really, I—"

"Take it, or I won't feel right asking you to bring us anything another time," Albion insisted. This being the case, Alex insisted Albion take his two pence change.

148

"And now, how about a glass of wine to wet your whistle?" Albion asked. "Or an ale, if you prefer."

"An ale would do the job," Alex agreed.

"I'm not a lover of the grape myself. Truth to tell, I like the grapes well enough, but it seems a pity they must destroy them by turning them into wine. I see the ladies narrowing their eyes at that notion," he laughed. "You gels go ahead—have wine, if you can stand the brackish taste of it."

The ladies had wine and sat nervously watching, praying their father would not give their noble caller a disgust of him. That they might institute some polite talk themselves did not occur to the mother and occurred to the daughters only to be rejected. Their fears proved unfounded. Before Penholme left, he had invited the whole family to the Hall for a short visit. They were astonished at the invitation, but not at all reluctant, and agreed to go in two days.

"You've thrown my household into a pelter, Penholme," Albion laughed. He considered the invitation no less than the prelude to an offer for one of his gels, but that Penholme scarcely glanced at Marilla made him think young Lord Robin was the best he might hope for. "The ladies will spend the night pawing through their wardrobes and their trinket boxes, deciding what gewgaws to wear."

"If they come just as they are, they will do you credit, sir," Alex said, smiling.

"I don't stint on dressing them up. A heifer is always brushed to a sheen before a show, as folks say," he declared with awful candor. Maggie gave an embarrassed smile.

A stray caller seldom got away from the Anglins' without having food pressed on him. A nobleman who issued an invitation was urged to remain to dinner, and when this was refused, a meal very much like a dinner was served on their laps as they sat at the sofa.

Alex made one more stop before going home. Remembering Albion's idea that Sawburne might be sold up to pay the arrears on Penholme's mortgage, he called on his solicitor and told him to draw up papers handing it over to Lord Robin. He was to take them to Penholme for signing the next morning. He hoped the Anglins' visit would result in an engagement between Maggie and Robin.

The visit caused Penholme's carriage to pass Rosedale after dark. As he was not expected back so soon, no eye was focused on the road in anticipation of his passing. He was tempted to stop, but bringing bad news to trouble sleep seemed inconsiderate. He went directly home to jog the servants into work for the pending visit from the Anglins.

Robin's first move after becoming an official landowner was to post over to Rosedale. Alex had not revealed the full extent of the situation in London, so the only news Robin brought was good news. Alex was home, and though he hadn't mentioned coming to Rosedale, he would certainly do so. Anne thought so, too, and rather wondered that he hadn't stopped the evening before.

"I didn't realize you were to get Sawburne so soon, Robin," Mrs. Wickfield said. "I thought it would be a year or so."

"Alex says I have shaped up so quickly he has no fear to let me run it myself. He brought the solicitor home with him and we signed the papers this very morning. The Anglins are coming to stay with us for a few days—Alex has given the nod to my offering for Maggie."

Lukewarm congratulations were offered.

"Mind, she hasn't said she'll have me, nor have I spoken to Albion. I don't relish that part of it, I can tell you."

"Is the whole family visiting, or just Miss Maggie?" Anne asked.

"The whole kit and caboodle. It's as good as a proposal—or an acceptance."

"Are you quite certain you want to offer for her?" Anne asked.

"Well, I think I do. I like her awfully, Annie, and was only waiting to hear what Alex and Rosie and everyone had to say about it, for it would be dashed uncomfortable having a bride no one would speak to. Alex thinks it's a capital idea, and, of course, Rosalie will be in alt. I daresay that's why Alex gave me Sawburne, so I'd have a roost to take my chick to."

And a rich father-in-law to pay off the mortgage, Anne silently added. That was Miss Maggie's great charm. But if Alex could afford to go through with giving Robin Sawburne, she might at least rest easy that the news in London had not been too horrid. She felt she would be receiving a visit herself soon and changed into her good blue mulled muslin to receive it. She put on her blue slippers with a wad of cotton to cushion the tacks, but no caller came.

By four in the afternoon, tempers at Rosedale were wearing thin. "That is odd," Mrs. Wickfield said. "I made sure we would hear from Alex by now. It's a pity I told Cook to prepare the green goose. I wouldn't have done it just for us."

Anne's hackles were lifting at such cavalier treatment. "He might at least have brought the brochure on the Carlton House table," she snipped.

Her mother stared at such foolishness but felt along with her daughter that Alex was developing a very odd kick in his gallop. A delay in the rendering of bad news she could understand, but the news in London was obviously good, so why didn't he come? The green goose was served and eaten. Twilight came and slowly receded into darkness.

By eight, Mrs. Wickfield's annoyance had escalated to a vague, unfocused anxiety. "Maybe one of the children is sick," she mentioned.

Anne's tone became more waspish as the evening progressed. "Robin would have told us. More likely Alex is riding herd on the servants, preparing the house for Anglin's visit," she said, sneering.

Mrs. Wickfield was unaccustomed to irony from her daughter and unwisely said, "Very likely that's it."

"I hope he doesn't have the gall to bring them here tomorrow," Anne said, and punched a pillow out of shape on the sofa beside her.

"My dear, he will bring them for a certainty. I'm glad you mentioned it. I must tell Cook to bake up some sweets. We must greet Robin's fiancée with respect. I hope he doesn't bring them for lunch. A tea we can manage with no trouble."

Anne hadn't a thing to say against Robin's fiancée, except that she was sister to Miss Anglin, preferred by Alex. She knew she could not treat the girl with friendliness, whatever about respect.

At Penholme, both the brothers and all the rest of the family were indeed in a bustle of activity to impress Robin's intended. There was much moving of furnishings and changing of linen and polishing of silver to remove the traces of decay. The Anglins arrived in state the next morning with four horses and two outriders. They came late in the morning, just before lunch, and after they had eaten, Robin undertook to amuse the ladies with a drive, while Albion entertained himself with an unguided tour of the house, where he busily reckoned up the worth of what he beheld. No pencil or paper was necessary for this procedure. His mind was like an abacus, keeping each figure in its proper column as he swiftly tallied up the value of paintings and furnishings and kept track of square footage of the Hall as he went along. He shook his head in wonder at a set of black rags hanging in a blue suite. Some family legend, very likely. If he heard a scream in the night or beheld a headless ghost parading the halls, he would know where it came from.

Left to his own devices, Penholme decided to test his wounded shoulder on his bay mare. His real aim was to be by himself for some more solitary thinking, but as all his troubles were being concealed from both guests and family till the visit was over, he claimed it was only a ride for pleasure and exercise.

Robin delivered the Anglin ladies to Rosedale, the first— the only—place that occurred to him, and sat down with all his usual familiarity to request a cup of tea. Mrs. Wickfield tried valiantly to conceal her daughter's coolness by an excess of friendly solicitude for her guests' preference for milk or lemon in their tea. She offered the macaroons and short cakes so often that even Maggie, a good eater, was replete. Anne was unhappy that Mrs. Anglin didn't saucer her tea or drop a single aitch that could be condemned. The sisters, especially Miss Anglin, behaved with such propriety that not a single charge of vulgarity could be raised against them. The worst to be said, and it was mere caviling, was that Miss Maggie had freckles—even they were confined to the bridge of her pretty little nose.

With a vast show of indifference, Anne finally brought herself to inquire of Robin, "Where are your brothers today?"

"Willie and Bung have gone trout fishing," he replied.

"She means Alex," Mrs. Wickfield explained bluntly.

"Alex has decided it is time to try his mount."

"He hasn't gone out on horseback with that arm!" Anne exclaimed.

"Yes, but his bay's a tame mount, and he promised to take it easy."

"You shouldn't have let him go!"

"Truth to tell, I thought he was only hacking down here," Robin said. "I was sure we'd find him with you. Has he not been to see you since he got back?"

"No, we haven't seen Penholme for a few days," Anne said coldly.

Robin noted the demeaning "Penholme" and wondered what could be the cause of it. Alex had been acting odd ever since his return. Obviously he and Annie had had a falling-out over something or other.

"If he ain't here, he's bound to be at the stream," he told her. "That's where he always goes when he wants to be alone."

"Fishing with the twins, you mean?"

"No, not the lake, the stream—the little creek that runs by the spinney. He always goes there to sulk, and he's been in a bad skin lately. I wish you would go and cheer him up."

"If he wants to be alone, then I shan't disturb him," Anne replied blandly, but it took all her fortitude to sit sipping tea after hearing this. She felt in her bones something was wrong. Something had happened in London.

Robin sensed her mood and soon ushered the guests out the door. Mrs. Wickfield turned a sapient eye on her daughter. "You'd better change into your habit. You don't want to get your second-best dress covered with horse hair and the stench of the stable."

Anne's chin assumed a mulish angle. "I am not riding today, Mama."

"Go on, ninnyhammer! Something happened in London. You'd best get busy and discover what it is."

"What has obviously happened is that Rosalie has convinced him to marry Miss Anglin. Why else are they visiting Penholme? Why else is he ashamed to come to see me?"

"The Anglins are there because Robin is marrying Maggie. I begin to wonder what has happened to your common sense, Annie. Now, get along with you, and don't come home without discovering what's ailing Alex, you hear!"

"I'm not going to chase after him."

"He might be lying on the cold ground with his wound bleeding for all you know. Go on, before I have to go myself."

With the pretext of an errand of mercy, Anne went so fast she left her good blue muslin lying in a heap on the floor and forgot to change her shoes.

When she found Penholme neither wounded nor bleeding but sitting calmly on a rock, staring into the stream, she felt foolish at having come pelting after him, the more so when he showed no pleasure at the interruption. In fact, he scowled quite openly, which threw her into a fit of indecision. Having come this far, she could hardly turn and leave without at least saying hello. She swallowed her pride and tried to make it look like a casual encounter.

"Oh, hello, Alex. I was just exercising Lady."

"How did you know I was here?" he asked, undeceived.

This cool question prevented her from dismounting. She remained aloft and stared down at him. "What makes you think I was looking for you? The day is so fine, I just came out for fresh air."

"I stand corrected. As you've accidentally stumbled onto me, why don't you stay awhile?"

Her impulse was to gallop away, but a closer inspection of his weary face softened her pique. There was clearly something very wrong. He offered a hand to help her dismount, but mindful of his shoulder, she clambered down by herself, wondering if a recrudescence of his old wound had him hipped.

"You shouldn't be riding so soon, should you? You mentioned a few weeks or a month. . . ."

"My arm's all right."

She knew by then the trouble was more than physical.

"I daresay you wonder that I haven't been to call," he said.

"No, Robin has just left. We do not hope to compete with rich merchants," she said, attempting an arch manner.

No smile or playful frown was returned, but a gloomy, grim silence. After a longish pause he said, "I've been meaning to call on you all day."

"Then I shall tell Mama we must just be patient a little longer." She walked to the rock and sat down, looking at the stream while waiting for an explanation of this fit of the dismals. Alex sat beside her, his fists rammed into the pockets of his trousers. He, too, stared into the running water.

"I take it things didn't go well in London," she finally said.

Alex turned his head and regarded her. His warm brown eyes held a new expression today, one she didn't immediately recognize. She thought at first he looked infinitely sad, but as she looked, the expression changed, became angry. "No, not well," he said curtly. "In fact, things couldn't be worse. We're finished. The London house is mortgaged—eight thousand on it."

"Oh, Alex! Surely not! Not on top of all the rest. That

156

must come to . . ." She tried to remember all the sums Charles had run through, but she got lost.

"It come to over fifty thousand he ran through, exclusive of his income," Alex said, and mentioned the various sources. "Another ten thousand from Uncle Cyrus—that one was new to me. Of course, there's a trifling five thousand more still in unpaid bills in London. Not to mention the little bit I have paid off in back salaries at home and the domestic bills in the village."

Anne sat dumbfounded at the list but no longer confused as to that unreadable face Alex wore. There was no way he could possibly cope with such a mountain of debt—all his properties gone or mortgaged and the income reduced. He hadn't come to see her because he had to tell her this. To tell her, in fact, that he couldn't marry her. He must marry Miss Anglin now, and obviously realized it himself. That was why the whole family was at Penholme. She sat silent, wearing an expression very much like him, though she didn't realize it. Totally disheartened at first, infinitely sad, then becoming angry as she realized that Charles was responsible for this debacle. Laughing, generous, flirtatious, handsome, damnable Charles.

Hot tears scalded her eyes. "I hate him," she said through clenched teeth.

Alex looked at her in surprise but not in doubt. "I've hated him for years," he said simply. "I tried not to. He was my brother, and I really tried very hard not to hate him, but to see him act so irresponsible while he threw our family's fortune to the winds, giving no heed to the children, no thought to his duties—to let Penholme and Sawburne go to rack and ruin. And to see him treat you so, Annie . . . I thought at least he meant to do the right thing by you."

"He did the right thing! He didn't marry me. I was

saved that humiliation, at least. How could I ever have . . . I was a young fool at the time." She dabbed a tear from the corner of her eye angrily, in a jerking fashion.

Alex reached out and patted her hand. "It's too bad I ever left. I should have stayed. I might have managed to do something with the ten thousand Uncle Cyrus left. Maybe if I'd been here sooner to take things in hand, I might have saved something."

"Don't blame yourself. It's not your fault. Oh, but I wish you hadn't gone, too, Alex."

"I had to make my own way in the world. I had nothing but the few thousand Mama left me, and it wasn't enough to buy a place. I wanted to become a colonel and come back and marry you. I had nothing to offer, Annie, when I finally began to suspect Charles didn't mean to marry you."

She looked at him in astonishment. "But you never looked at me! You didn't care for me at all."

"Oh, Duck!" He laughed ruefully. "How could I bear to look at you, pining for Charles, seeing your eyes follow him as though he were a demigod, knowing he had so much to offer—looks, money, title. I couldn't stand it. I avoided you both as much as I could. Then when Charles began to speak of marrying an heiress—after one of my almighty harangues—I took the notion that if I became a hero—a sort of superior Wellington was what I had in mind—you might be impressed enough to have me. Or alternatively, on cloudy days, I thought I might fall in some vastly heroic death, with the corollary, of course, that you would come to appreciate me after I was gone. I daresay you never realized your role in the case was to don crepe and live a life of solitary regret."

"Oh, I wish . . ." she said futilely.

"When they brought me the news of Charles's death in

158

Spain, I was half delirious in Belem, but the first thought that ran through my fevered brain wasn't that my brother was dead or that I was now Lord Penholme. It was that there was no possibility of your marrying Charles. You were free, and I'd come home and marry you. It's all that kept me alive, Annie. It was a dreadful mistake on my part to have ever enlisted. I knew it as soon as I got there. I was no hero, but I was there, with no place else to go, so I stayed. When I got back, I thought it was the end of all my troubles. A little penny-pinching, cheese-paring, and we could get married. I soon realized you were in love with a ghost. Weren't you?''

"With a sham. I had no idea what he was really like.''

"I almost wish we hadn't come so close,'' he said, then his voice broke. He looked away toward the stream with his jaw clenched. It was unfitting for an officer to have moist eyes.

Such bravery was not required of a woman. Anne sniffled quite audibly into her handkerchief.

"Don't cry, Annie,'' he said, which made the tears come faster. He put an arm around her shoulder, and her head drooped against his chest while she tried to dry her tears and compose herself. His arm tightened around her; she felt some pressure on her head from his fingers or lips. She thought that perhaps he had kissed the top of her head, and she looked up.

"Alex, I have five thousand, if that's any help . . .''

"Don't, Duck,'' he said unsteadily. "Prices are still going up. You'll need it for buying tacks and thread. I can't marry you. To know you would have had me—that will have to be enough.''

"It's *not* enough!'' she objected. "You shouldn't have given Robin Sawburne. If Charles was too selfish, you're too generous.''

"It wasn't just idle generosity. I would have lost it anyway. Anglin will bail him out, and we'll have a home in the family. Somewhere for the children to go if I have to leave."

"Leave? Alex, you're not rejoining the army!" she gasped.

"Lord, no! I didn't mean that. I'd sooner live in hell. I'm thinking of setting up as a diplomat, as soon as I find out what it pays. I speak some Spanish and Portuguese now, though I'd prefer any other posting to Spain. Austria, maybe. I'll be as bad a diplomat as I was a soldier, but at least I won't be required to kill anyone."

Anne drew her bottom lip between her teeth and began imagining herself as a diplomatic hostess. "That might not be so bad," she said, a hopeful question lighting her face.

"It will be wretched! I'll be away from you."

"Oh! Can—can they not be married?"

"Only if they have the effrontery to ask a woman to marry them, without a sou to their names. I haven't. You can do better for yourself than a maimed pauper, and an exile at that," he said firmly. "Forget about me, Annie. It's all over for us. We must both do what we can to set our lives to rights."

"Would you be able to save Penholme if you took the job?"

"At the moment, it's only a possibility. I haven't begun to look into it yet. But even if I could hold on to it, I couldn't look after the tenants. There are more people than just family to consider, darling. I fear for the health of my tenants, living in damp, drafty cottages, barely eking a living out of the land."

"Then you'll be returning to London."

"I must. There are a dozen loose ends to tie up there."

"You'll call on me when you get back this time?" she asked.

"Yes, if you like."

"Even if the news is bad, Alex. Don't leave me in suspense again."

"I'll tell you, but really, Anne, the news isn't likely to be good. Don't raise your hopes."

The weak little shoot of hope that had been trying to sprout shriveled at this blast, and she looked at him disconsolately. "It would have been so nice. Alex, there is always Rosedale. . . ."

"Not always. Only while your mama is alive. No, Annie, I don't want it to be like that. Penholme is my home and my family's home. It has been for generations. I must save it, if at all possible."

"But what will you do?"

A fierceness possessed him; it echoed in his voice when he answered. "Whatever I have to." He looked deeply into her eyes—an angry look, it was. Then he removed his arm from around her shoulders and rose.

He thought of the London house, well furnished. That lumber should bring a few thousand at auction. Sell the house as well—two thousand would be realized after the mortgage was paid. He also thought of Annie's five thousand, hating the necessity of doing it, but it could be done. Exmore and the merchants were consigned a long wait for their money. He'd strip Penholme of all but the basic necessities of life. They'd live in an empty house, if necessary. Sell every stick of lumber, every inch of canvas, every piece of silver, every spare piece of horseflesh in the stable. He hadn't come through three years of hell, miraculously surviving a wound that everyone thought fatal, finally found Annie loved him enough to go into exile with him, only to be defeated again by Charles. He'd marry her if they had to live in the dovecot.

"Whatever I have to," he repeated softly, fiercely, then turned away.

"You're leaving now?"

"Yes, but I'll be back," he said on a determined note. "Good-bye, Duck."

He mounted and rode away. Anne remained sitting at the stream for a long while, remembering Alex's words and the determined way he had uttered them. Whatever he had to do . . . He was going to marry Miss Anglin, then, and she couldn't even blame him. She threw a pebble into the stream and watched it sink. Of course, things sank when their weight was too much to be borne. Everything sank in the end—hopes, wishes, love.

Chapter Thirteen

There was a delightful piece of news awaiting Lord Penholme when he returned to the Hall. Robin had offered for Miss Maggie and had been accepted. Albion was impatiently pacing the front hall when Penholme arrived, and he whisked his host into the study to discuss settlements before that gentleman had time to wash his hands. Alex felt a stirring of apprehension at having to disclose the true state of affairs to the man. He would not have been the least surprised to have him call off when the whole morass of bills was divulged, but at least Robin was clear of the debts. He had only the Sawburne mortgage to worry about.

"Now," Albion said blissfully, "if we was to put your goods on one hand and your debts on t'other, just where would you stand?" A pair of eyes of a daunting craftiness regarded his lordship sharply.

"We would stand pretty well on one foot," Penholme said. "The wrong one, I fear. But Robin is better situated than I."

"We'll start with the Hall—only ten thousand clear there, and another ten thousand in furnishings, I make it. So there's twenty thousand on the right side—the credit side."

Penholme brightened to hear such a high estimate placed

on his chattels. Another five thousand was consigned to the right side by the unseen furnishings in the London house. "It is the custom to assess the town furnishings at fifty percent of country goods," Albion mentioned. Penholme was too cheered to quibble. He owned up manfully to the London mortgage. "I feared I might be right on that score," Albion said modestly.

Penholme did not feel it necessary to say he owed Exmore close to five thousand.

"Then there's the holdings assembled by the late lords of Penholme," Albion rattled on.

Feeling any holdings Charles had a hand in were more likely to have been disbursed than assembled, Penholme spoke reluctantly. "I haven't gone through my brother's papers. I have them in my room to look over tonight."

Albion stared at such a dilatory way of going on. "There'll be holdings there," he said hopefully. It was not mentioned that the holdings were mostly in a worthless shipbuilding company. "You have a while to run an eye over them before dinnertime," Albion added impatiently.

There would clearly be no hiding anything from this inquisitor, but the burden was Alex's, not Robin's. For that matter, Albion might be the very one to advise him how to go on. "Would you like to have a look at them now, sir?" he suggested.

Albion's broad smile hardly required any verbal confirmation, but he said, "I'd be happy to have a glance at them with you."

"I have to wash up, but if . . ."

"I daresay I could work faster alone."

The boxes of bills and "holdings" were handed over to the merchant, who settled into Penholme's study with a smile of anticipation at getting such exact and voluminous information to play with. He was given a box of cigars and a pot of tea, for Albion never befuddled his mind with spirits when he was ciphering. "You needn't bother holding dinner for me. A chop on a plate here at the desk will do fine," he said, rubbing his hands in pleasure at the delightful evening ahead of him.

The meal was a happy one in spite of Albion's absence. Robin was radiant, and Miss Maggie in alt. Miss Anglin foresaw a considerable increase in the new beaux to whom she would be exposed as a result of her sister's alliance, and even Mrs. Anglin said without a word of prompting that she was very happy for the match, very happy indeed. And so she was. Lord Robin was very easy to talk to when he wasn't with his family. He rattled on so merrily that she hardly had to say a word.

After the customary gulping of the port, Penholme and Robin joined the ladies in the gold saloon, but still Albion remained shut up in the smoky office, nodding his head as he toted up long columns. The Misses Anglin helped pass the evening by playing and singing for the family, and the twins brought down their war trophies to be admired. Mrs. Anglin sought company in the young girls, Loo and Babe, and became quite talkative for the half hour they were allowed to visit. At nine, the children were sent to bed, but still no word came from the study.

Penholme became apprehensive when the clock showed ten and still silence prevailed from that quarter. He feared Albion had changed his mind and disliked to tell him. Unable to control his curiosity longer, he went to the study door on the pretext of seeing if his guest wanted fresh tea. He could scarcely see Albion for the smoke, but amid the blue clouds, the grizzled head still leaned over ruler-straight columns of figures, with a pencil flying up and down at an incredible speed.

"I'll be with ye shortly," Albion said without looking

up. He certainly wore a frown, but whether of horror or merely concentration, Alex could not ascertain.

The Anglin ladies and Aunt Tannie retired at eleven, and with a yawn, Robin said he, too, was ready for the tick. Penholme took a cigar out to the garden. The lights of Rosedale were visible in the distance, nestled there in the valley. From the nettles beyond, the sweet song of nightingales echoed. He watched silently as the lights were extinguished one by one, first downstairs, then above. Annie's was the last to go out. He smiled sadly in the warm darkness, his heart tender to think of her offering him her five thousand pounds and even a home at Rosedale. The four children would have to sleep in the attic—and what would the whole countryside think? No, it was impossible, but the offer touched him.

He might let Penholme Hall and hire a smaller place, though. If Albion's conclusion was very bad, he could do that. He stayed for some time in the garden, thanking God he was home safe, if not quite sound. His shoulder was healing quickly now. How fortunate he hadn't let that Spanish sawbones hack off his arm. A shiver convulsed him with the memory of that period. What was being bankrupt compared with that? At length he returned to the saloon and had a glass of wine while waiting for the verdict.

It was five minutes to twelve when Albion came, carrying in his fingers a clutch of figured papers. "Your brother was an expensive lad," he said, shaking his head. "I've never heard a harsh word against him, but he was shockingly dear."

Alex's throat constricted. "Yes," he said in a high, unnatural tone. It was disaster, then.

Albion laid the papers on a table and rubbed his hands in satisfaction at a job well done. "I daresay you're anxious to know what you're worth if you was to be sold up," he said.

"Very anxious." So much so that his palms were moist and his tongue was bone-dry.

"I make it fifty thousand even," Albion announced.

Penholme stared in disbelief. "Fifty thousand! There must be some mistake."

"I don't make mistakes," Albion said, not boasting but simply stating an immutable fact. "It's your holdings that have led you astray. You thought you was good for a little more, I daresay, but your shipping stocks—worth nothing. He lost a tidy sum on that one. Ten thousand three hundred pounds and some odd shillings and pence. Six shillings, four pence, if you want the exact sum." He didn't even have to consult his ciphering to come up with it. "I could have warned him away from shipping. However . . ."

"Fifty thousand, you say?" Penholme asked, still unable to believe it.

"Aye, fifty-five at today's quotation, less the five in duns from London merchants. Actually four thousand, five hundred. It's a great pity about the shipping outfit. He should have known with a brother in the army that war's no time for shipping stocks. But that's the way with the market: you win some: you lose some."

Penholme looked for enlightenment. It seemed some considerable sum had been won to have pulled him out of debt. "How about the other holdings?" he asked.

"It's your gas company stocks that saved your bacon. Without your Gas, Light and Coke Company shares, you'd be in the suds for sure. He doubled his investment there, from fifteen thousand to thirty. It more than makes up for your shipping shares. A great pity to think of that waste. If he'd put the lot into the gas shares—but it's done. Too

167

late to cry over it now." He looked ready to shed a tear all the same.

"Gas company stocks?" Penholme said, feeling like one in a dream, afraid to think lest he should awaken.

"Aye, I'm into them heavily myself. I'm just wondering whether it isn't time to divest and get into something else. The fast, easy money has been made, though they might be good for a boost awhile yet. Do you plan to hold on to yours, Penholme?"

"No."

"I figured if I myself was in your boots I'd sell out and pay down those mortgages. Stocks are for money you don't need, for as sure as ever you have to cash them in, they'll be down. Not to say you ought to pay off the whole mortgage. What I'd do if I was you is knock Penholme down to a manageable size—say, twenty—and hold on to a bit of blunt to look after work that needs doing. Your tenant farms, for instance, are . . . depreciating," he said with an unusual discretion. "But don't let yourself run right up against the wall. Keep a sum on hand, for if you invest it all, you'll discover a sudden need for cash, and pay out a stiff interest for it. Now, as to your London place, will you be wanting the use of it right away?"

Penholme, storing up every golden syllable, said, "No. Do you think I should sell?"

Albion stared. "Oh, sell? Never sell such a sterling investment as that. Berkeley Square—money in the bank. It'll do nothing but become more valuable with the passing of the years. If the roof fell in, the land it stands on alone would be worth a fortune. I'm looking out for a couple of properties in the West End myself. But if you won't be using it, what you could do to cut a corner is let it furnished to some decent soul that won't destroy it on you. Let strangers pay off your mortgage with their rents. As good a way as any to build up a tidy sum. What I do myself is put a down payment on a place just big enough that the rents cover the mortgage and upkeep, then I sit back and let others buy my houses for me. As simple as A, B, C. I don't know why more folks don't do the same."

"I can't imagine," Alex said, seeing that some reply was wanted and saying what required the least effort. In his heart, he was not standing in the saloon with Albion at all. He was tearing down the hill to Rosedale to tell Annie the news. He thought she might be lying in her bed this very minute, worrying, as indeed she was.

"Now as to Lord Robin and that chit of mine," Albion said, "I'll pay off his little mortgage so that he and Maggie ain't strapped starting off. Not that it would do them a bit of harm. Me and Minnie lived in a cold garret for two years while we were saving up our nest egg, and thrived like a patch of weeds. When Marilla came along, it was time to move into one of our houses."

That a man should live in a cold garret with his wife while he apparently owned better establishments was a way of proceeding that brought Penholme to interested attention. "Really?" he asked.

"Aye, we agreed to it beforehand. But with your brother being a lord, it won't be his way of going on, and not in the least necessary, either. With no mortgage, he'll be able to keep his income of three thousand, and with Maggie's dowry—I plan to make it twenty-five thousand, if ye've no objection, they'll be able to handle their simple needs."

"I have no objection," Penholme said promptly.

"I thought you might want a trifle more. If Lord Robin objects . . ."

"He won't."

"Ye'll not be bear-leading the lad much longer. But no doubt ye've talked it over together. It's only natural.

169

Twenty-five, I figure, is a fair price for a younger son. It's the going rate, at least. Now, if it was you we was discussing, of course, the figure would be somewhat higher. Say, fifty thousand . . .''

Penholme swallowed a smile to hear Robin being bought up so disinterestedly, as though he were a horse or bull. He hastily assured Albion that he himself was not for sale, though, of course, he worded it more discreetly and made sure to add a word of praise on Miss Anglin.

''Yer sister, the duchess, mentioned a match between you and my chit. I couldn't help noticing myself you was making mighty large eyes at the Wickfield lady. She'd have a tidy dowry, I daresay.''

''Not large,'' Penholme confessed, seeing there would be no keeping any financial secrets from this in-law. ''There has been an understanding between us for some time.''

''No need to apologize, milord. None in the least. I daresay you was only the younger son when your da arranged the deal, but being a man of honor, you'll stand by it. We've got the connection with the family now, and my daughter will be meeting any number of fine lords. Happen you'd have one to recommend, a cousin or what will you?''

''My sister is the one to advise you. She would be delighted to do it.''

''I'll keep an eye peeled as well. Marilla's getting on. Nearly twenty, though she don't like me saying so. It'll go against the pluck, Maggie beating her to the altar, but it's for the best. It'll throw her on to the right path. Just between you and me and the stovepipe, I do think she's got a touch more class than Maggie. She speaks proper and all that, wouldn't you say?''

''An unexceptionable girl. Lady!'' Penholme assured his guest.

Albion smiled in benign contentment. "She is, nearly."
He smiled.

"This calls for a toast," Penholme said, beaming from
ear to ear and wanting to shout and laugh for pure joy.

Albion thought the matter for jubilation was the marriage, for it would never have occurred to him that a man
would know by less than three or four pounds what he was
worth. Penholme forgot, in his joy, that Albion didn't drink
wine, and Albion manfully held his breath and drank a
swallow without complaint.

"We forgot to include your wine cellar, by Jove!" was
his comment. "I daresay this is considered a good brew."

"The Penholme cellars are famous. Both my father and
my brother paid a good deal of attention to them. I must
own I haven't been downstairs since I came home."

"You certainly ought to have a look!" Albion said rather
testily. "I daresay there are family jewels and such things
we ought to have included, too."

"Yes, some rather fine heirlooms, but they are entailed."

"I only made a rough estimate." He mentally added ten
thousand to the proper side of the ledger. He didn't want
to declare his new connections as being worth a penny less
than they were when he spread the word in London of the
match he had arranged. The first merger would set the basis
for the second, and it was important that the next set of in-
laws measure up to the Penholmes.

"We'll hop over to Sawburne tomorrow, if you don't
mind. I'm anxious to look the place over. Then we'll arrange the wedding party. Maggie will want a stylish do.
I'll rig her out fine as a star. Don't be backward in asking
any of your family and friends to it. The more the merrier.
It will throw Marilla in the way of worthwhile suitors. I
daresay the duchess is the very one could give Minnie a

hand with the spread. Could she be lured to my mansion to pay us a visit, do you think? We'd do up the food and all just as she orders. She could bring any number of servants so she'd feel at home."

Rosalie approved of the match, and might very well enjoy such a novel holiday as visiting the Anglins. In any case, he was able to assure Albion that his sister would not miss the wedding.

Albion soon retired to his chamber, to tell this news to his wife, who was terrified to hear it. "Ye'll have to take yourself by the scruff of the neck and face it, love," he told her kindly. "It's what we agreed between us we wanted for the girls. Ye'll get on to their ways in no time. They're not at all a bad lot when you get to know them. Why, you and Lord Robin are already as friendly as thieves, and ye'll like Penholme, too, when you talk to him. Besides, it ain't him we'll be visiting but our own Maggie and Lord Robin, and he is a jolly young gumboil."

Minnie squared her thin shoulders to this new task. She saw no injustice in having worked and saved all her life, to have in her declining years the privilege of paying hard cash for a life she dreaded, amid people who frightened her half to death. She had been beguiled by Lord Robin some weeks ago, and she thought that with his help she could face the rest of the family.

Penholme took his guest's sheets of accounting and the precious boxes of holdings to his room and went over them closely, to assure himself it was not a dream. There were sheafs and sheafs—a whole box of documents—relating to the Gas, Light, and Coke Company. Charles had actually done some research before investing. It was odd he hadn't told Rosalie about these shares, but she would have insisted he sell them to pay Exmore—or possibly tried to cadge some of the money from him. Yes, it was wise to keep the secret. The date of the purchase was shortly after Alex had left for the Peninsula. Charles had felt some remorse, then—the argument and the awful decision to leave had borne some good fruit. A further investigation showed the mortgage on the London residence was used to buy the ship stocks. Charles must have borrowed the rest, which accounted for some of his huge expenditures.

With all this before him, Alex was able to forgive his brother a good deal. He quit hating Charles that night and felt a stab of regret that they had parted on such bad terms. Though if they hadn't fought . . . It was typical of Charles that he would try to recoup the family fortune by a risky investment, but at least one of his schemes had come through, and it was impossible to hate him after that.

Alex didn't even try to sleep till after two. It was past three when he finally closed his eyes. He had, in the interim, told Annie the news, gotten engaged, married, and moved her into Penholme—all in his mind. The only future part of his life not decided upon was what to do with Aunt Alice. Whether she should come to Penholme with them or stay on at Rosedale must be her own decision. How pleasant it was, that two suitable alternatives should be available to Anne's mother.

Chapter Fourteen

Anne returned from the meeting with Alex completely unstrung. She told her mother what had happened, then went to her room for a short, violent bout of tears. By dinner, she had assumed a veneer of composure that allowed her to move the food about on her plate; swallowing was impossible. They went together to the saloon to discuss the situation, with Mrs. Wickfield assuring her daughter that it was by no means hopeless. If worse came to worst, the whole family could move into Rosedale, and that would be a deal better than Alex going abroad as an ambassador.

Anne thought so, too, but the memory of that chin squaring up and the determined light in Alex's eye when he declared he would do whatever he had to to keep Penholme unnerved her. There was Miss Anglin at the Hall, and Alex liked her. With Robin marrying Miss Maggie, a second marriage in the same family would be easy to slip into. Really from every aspect except her own romantic one, it was the wise thing to do. Her mother poo-pooed the notion, but in her heart Anne was afraid the inevitable would occur. Not today, not tomorrow—Alex was too considerate for that—but eventually he would marry Miss Anglin.

Talking was better than keeping it all bottled up inside, and the ladies talked till late into the night, then went to bed to think about what they had said and try to figure a way out of the muddle. Mrs. Wickfield was up early, haggard from lack of sleep, but she always rose with the chickens, whether she had slept or not. It was still early when Penholme stopped on his way to London.

"Robin has taken the Anglins over to Sawburne, and I'm off to London," he said, smiling widely. "Where's Annie? I must talk to her at once."

Mrs. Wickfield had never seen Alex so excited. She looked in shock at the almost hysterically happy man before her. "She didn't get to sleep till all hours. I don't like to waken her, Alex. You seem in mighty high spirits."

"I am, Auntie. You'll never guess what happened."

"What?" she asked eagerly.

"I'm rich. Can't you waken Annie? I must talk to her."

"Rich? How?"

"It's a miracle. Albion did it—I love him," he said, and, tossing up his hands, laughed like a deranged man.

"Albion?"

"Yes, he gave me a hand last night, went through my papers, and made me a rich man. Did I tell you I'm off to London?"

"You're going to sell the house—is that it?"

"What, sell a sterling investment? Why, it would still be worth a king's ransom if the roof fell in. He told me not to sell. I mean to follow Albion's advice in everything. I'm stopping at Exmore's place to make Rosalie come and visit my new in-laws."

"But what happened, Alex? How did Albion make you rich?"

"Really, it was Charles who did it. It's all very complicated. He wasn't such a bad brother after all. How could

175

he know his ship would sink? At least the gas stocks didn't blow up. Albion is heavily into gas stocks.''

He rattled on so disjointedly that she hardly knew what to make of it. ''Gas stocks, you say?''

''Yes, they have to be sold now. I want to do it before they go down.'' He looked impatiently at his watch. ''Perhaps I won't wait for Annie to get up. Let her sleep. But tell her not to worry and not to pack her bags to go abroad either. With Albion's help, I've saved Penholme. You're invited to the wedding, by the way. Albion is planning a capital do.''

''What wedding is this, Alex?'' she asked fearfully.

''Oh, Robin's and Maggie's, of course. They will go first.''

''Perhaps I should rouse her.''

''No, don't bother. I am anxious to get to London and settle everything. It would take her a while to get dressed. I'll leave but be back tomorrow. Isn't it wonderful? Really, we were foolish to look down our noses at the Anglins. They're very nice.''

He walked to the door, still rattling on in a fashion that made little sense. But two facts emerged clearly: he had saved Penholme, and the Anglins were very much involved. His happiness proved contagious. Mrs. Wickfield hummed as she went about her duties, and when Anne came downstairs sometime later, her eyes heavy, she was surprised to see such happy spirits bubbling out of her mama.

''Alex has been here'' she was told, and, of course, the rest of the story soon came out.

Anne was first ecstatic, then curious, and finally doubtful. ''But what did Anglin do, exactly?''

''I don't understand it, my dear. Alex was very excited. It has something to do with Charles.''

176

"I find that hard to believe."

"And gas stocks and a ship that sank. Did I tell you Alex is bringing Rosalie to visit the Anglins?"

Rosalie's presence at this time was nothing but a disaster. "The Anglins? Why not the Hall?"

"I don't know, Anne. As I said, Alex was strangely excited. A kind of euphoria—or hysteria," she added uncertainly.

Exactly how Penholme was to be saved was unclear, and Anne soon began to wonder whether Anglin had convinced Alex to marry Miss Anglin. Her mother declared it was no such a thing. He wouldn't have been wearing a smile from ear to ear if that were the case, now would he?

Anne could not think he would, but why else should Anglin settle his debts for him? Her mother obviously misunderstood something that had been said. There was no way in the world Charles had helped from the grave. All his acts while alive had been disastrous. It was too exciting a mystery to continue for a whole day, so the ladies loaded into the gig and went to Penholme to talk to Aunt Tannie, from whom they learned exactly nothing.

The whole household had been up and gone before she had come to breakfast. When she had gone to bed the night before, Anglin had been locked up in the study with Alex's papers, and when she had come down, everyone was gone, so she ended up exacting information instead of giving it. She was questioned closely as to what degree of intimacy existed between Miss Anglin and Alex, and had to confess he seemed to like her pretty well. Most damning of all, he had been seen walking with her in the orchard at some unremembered time. The ladies returned home no wiser than when they had left, to face an afternoon and evening of uncertainty.

In London, Alex was much more happily occupied selling his shares in the Gas, Light and Coke Company, giving Naismith money to discharge Charles's debts, paying Rosalie, and finding a tenant for the London house. As he couldn't get so much done in one day, he stayed part of the next, rather than have to return. He was finished by afternoon, but so late that the wiser course was to stay overnight.

In a mellow mood, he was induced to pay his respects to Aunt Lucretia. He made a hit there, for he was an ex-officer, even if he didn't wear his scarlet tunic. When he politely declined an offer of a loan, Lucretia was so stunned, she quite insisted he take ten guineas as a gift. Rosalie, who accompanied him, railed like a harpy at his stupidity. "You should have read her a Cheltenham tragedy, for she would certainly have offered to bail you out." But he left a good impression behind, so that there was some possibility his stupidity might yet bring a reward when the will was read.

He told Rosalie all his plans and got her agreement to visit the Anglins before the wedding. Indeed, she quite looked forward to it, though she could not go for a few days. "What a lark! I would love it, of all things. Bertie will be wearing a face like thunder. I'll billet half a dozen servants on Albion to impress him. They will be willing to spend any amount. It would be a pity to have it vulgar, when a little help from me could do it up in style. Besides, I cannot allow the bride to outblaze me in her gown. And how about your wedding, Alex? Will it be first?"

"Annie will decide, but it will be very soon."

"She'll run you to the altar before you have time for a second thought. Of course, I couldn't be happier for you."

"I know," he said. "I only wish Charlie could be here."

"But if he were, you would not be marrying her, would you?" she asked with no notion of giving offense.

"Do you know, sis, I think I would," he said contentedly.

Rosalie smiled politely and uttered not a word of enlightenment.

Penholme ordered from Weston a blue coat of Bath cloth
and a formal suit for his wedding. A curled beaver hat,
gloves, and a walking stick were put into his possession
on Bond Street. Rosalie did not consider him elegant
enough yet that she insisted he accompany her to a party,
but he was happier to stay home. He planned to leave early
the next morning. He made only two stops before going,
one to retrieve the family heirlooms from the London vault.
He would not return to London soon and wanted Anne to
have the jewelry on her wedding day. The last stop was to
buy six yards of white crepe. He had no idea what quantity
was required for a gown, but six yards looked enough for
anything.

As the carriage bolted through the spring countryside,
he alternately smiled and laughed aloud, all alone in the
carriage, as he hastened to Penholme.

His staying another day did nothing to ease exacerbated
nerves at Rosedale. Aunt Tannie came to call the second
afternoon, to say that the party at Sawburne was remaining
overnight. As Alex was expected home that day, no eye
was long turned from the front window that would give a
view of any carriage passing on the road. Each was scru-
tinized carefully, but none was Penholme's. After two cups
of tea, Aunt Tannie left, shaking her head and hoping in a
despondent fashion that Alex hadn't done something foolish, by which she meant—and they all knew it—something
wise, like offering for Miss Anglin.

Early the next morning, the Wickfields resumed their
vigil at the window. By afternoon, they knew every branch
and leaf on the mulberry tree by heart. They knew they

had to bend their heads to see the farthest corner of the road. It was approaching teatime when Penholme's carriage passed Rosedale. It passed and did not turn in as the watchers felt confident it would. The women looked at each other, doubt stiffening their faces.

"I don't like the looks of this," Mrs. Wickfield worried.

"He is anxious to get to the Hall to see Miss Anglin," Anne said, and looked hopefully for contradiction.

"No such a thing. He wants to freshen up—that's all. And you know, Annie, it was never his way to come down just at mealtime. He'll have a bite and be here in an hour or two. Why, the Anglins aren't even at the Hall."

"He doesn't know that. Besides, they must be back by now."

"Pshaw! You make me angry with your gloomy notions. He wouldn't have said not to worry if he'd offered for Miss Anglin, would he?"

"You're *sure* he said that?"

"Certainly he did. And in such a way, with his eyes shining. He'll be here before you can say Jack Robinson. Go brush up your hair and put on a ribbon to be ready for him."

Anne felt an unbearable churning of excitement. She not only brushed her hair but made a very distracted toilette, to pass the time till Alex arrived. Tea was forgotten entirely at this crucial moment. His carriage was so soon rolling up to the door, however, that it was clear he hadn't stopped to eat. In fact, he had done no more than clean away the dust of travel and put on a fresh shirt and cravat. He had, for the sake of civility, to say a word to the Anglins, who had just arrived from Sawburne.

"Are you going to see Annie now?" Robin asked.

"Yes," Alex said, walking briskly to the door.

"Let me go with you. I want to see her face."

"I don't think . . . Oh, very well," Alex agreed, too happy to say no to anyone. "But don't be sticking to us like a burr after we get there. Give us some privacy."

Miss Maggie, never long from Robin's side, also hopped out to the carriage. "Come on, Marilla," she called to her sister. Marilla was under orders to ingratiate herself with every lady and gentleman possible, so she, too, went with them. It was a jolly trip. Alex had given Robin a fine ring for his bride. No one knew it had been purchased by Charles with Harriet Wilson in mind, or wondered how such an important piece was unentailed.

When the carriage was finally close enough to be seen from Rosedale's saloon window, Mrs. Wickfield called her daughter, who came pelting down the stairs in such a rush she tripped and very nearly broke her neck. Her eyes widened in dismay to discern the Anglin ladies within the carriage.

"He had the temerity to bring her here!" Anne whispered, aghast. Her eyes flew to the stairway as she wondered whether she had time to get up it before they were in. She hadn't. Alex bounded up the steps two at a time and pounced in without knocking, to enter the saloon ten steps ahead of the others. The ladies scarcely had time to turn from the window. Alex took a quick step toward Anne, then halted as he saw Mrs. Wickfield by her side. Robin and the girls were just coming in the front door with all the accompanying racket of a group of healthy youngsters.

"Where can we hide?" Alex asked. He grabbed Anne by one hand. She noticed that in the other he clutched a brown parcel. "Can you stave off the bunch, Auntie?" he asked. "We'll be with you directly."

No stranger to Rosedale, he wasn't long finding a hiding spot in the morning parlor. He closed the door, tossed the parcel on a table, and released Anne's hand. He stood looking silently at her for a long minute with a very happy, triumphant, intense look on his face.

"We've done it, Annie." Her doubts vanished when she saw him there, looking at her as if she were a jewel beyond price. "By God, we've done it."

Without further waste of time or words, she ran into his arms, all doubts and fears abandoned. She was kissed with a very satisfying violence. "I never thought . . ." he began to say, but was soon kissing her again, hungrily and with renewed vigor.

During a pause for air, Anne said, "Alex, you haven't told me . . ." His lips brushed hers to silence.

"Later," he mumbled in a dazed voice, and kissed her again, crushing her against him in a way that promised harm to his wound.

"Alex, do be careful," she cautioned in a breathless voice.

"I've been careful all my life, Duck. Too cautious. I should have done this three years ago."

"Yes, but—"

"No buts." He kissed her again gently, then pressed her head against his shoulder. "We have three lost years to make up. How soon can we start?"

"Alex, you haven't told me *anything.*"

"Didn't your mama tell you?"

"Only that Albion had helped you somehow, and . . ."

"Albion is the one who discovered it." He went on to tell her all about that evening of revelation. "So Charles wasn't quite the wastrel we've been thinking him. We don't hate him anymore, do we? Really, I hated hating him."

"I'm ready to love him—and the Anglins—the whole world."

"Say you love *me;* you can't think how I've longed to hear you say it."

"You, most of all. That goes without saying."

"I'm so happy I could fly. Shall we take off into the blue, Duck? Fly home to Penholme, our Penholme."

"I'd love it, but should we not waddle into the saloon first and say good day to our darling in-laws? No, I am not being satirical! If their blunt is good enough for us, so is their blood. I only disliked them because I thought you meant to offer for Marilla."

"I—Marilla?" he asked, brown eyes blinking. "Annie, you must know I've never looked at any girl but you. I must be the most faithful lover that ever was. All the time you were dangling after Charles, I was constant as marble. Not even in Spain, with all those dark-eyed señoritas following the drum. I never wanted anyone but you, Duck, in my whole life. Since I was old enough to think of such things—and you were much too young—I've been waiting for you."

"I—I didn't think you loved her, but I knew you must redeem Penholme. You said you would do anything. I daresay Albion would have come down heavy for an earl."

"Fifty thousand was the sum mentioned," he admitted, smiling at the memory.

"Oh, she's worth ten times as much as I am!"

"Not to me. I wish he had offered a million, that it might have seemed a real temptation. But it wouldn't have been. Nothing would. What is money for but to gain security and happiness? You are my happiness. We'll be as inseparable as Juno's swans. I have you, and we have Penholme. Money is irrelevant."

"How strange that sounds, after what we've been through."

"I'm irrational with joy. Money matters a great deal, of course, especially when you don't have it. I intend to run a tight ship at home, to see we don't run into the shoals of bankruptcy again. Be prepared with your hammer and tacks to shore up the family footgear.''

"Are we really out of deep waters?"

"Sailing free. A lot of work to be done still, but I relish that. I have plans to ship the excess of servants out to Sawburne—they can afford anything there, the nabobs.''

"I personally will gladly forgo my white crepe gown for a few years. I want to do my bit.''

"We aren't that poor, Anne. You are to be my one extravagance. I mean to see you turned out in style. I have new outfits coming up from Weston. I can't have my style ruined by wearing a dowd on my arm. Family tradition must be maintained, and we Penholmes have a strong streak of the peacock. To get you started, I have brought you something from London.''

He took the brown parcel from the table and pulled it open, with a quite careless disregard for the paper, which with careful handling could have been reused. Yards of creamy crepe flowed from his fingers. He draped a corner around her neck, and she turned in circles, laughing, to wrap it around her body.

"Alex, such waste! There are yards too much!''

"I want you to have too much of everything, just as you would have if you had married Charles.''

"Yes, too much drinking and gambling and debts—to say nothing of mistresses!''

He grabbed her fingers and pulled her to him, his eyes glowing. "I'll make you a better husband than he would have, Annie. Truly, I will. I'm not as tall or handsome or as dashing. My poor old carcass is full of holes, but I love you better than anyone else in the world ever could.''

A lump rose in her throat at this heartfelt speech. "I know. We've agreed not to hate Charles; now shall we agree to forget him? He wasn't as bad as we thought—

since he happened to get lucky and regain a little of the money he lost. You are more handsome and more dashing to me. And you are rapidly getting taller, too. I love you better than I ever loved him, Alex. Isn't that what you really want to know?''

"Thank you, my darling Duck. That is exactly what I wanted to hear you say. I already felt it, but my ears wanted to hear it, too," he said in a loving voice. "I shan't pester you with my doubts again. Now we'll unwind you from this marriage shroud and go do the pretty with the in-laws. You chose wisely, by the way. The white crepe does enhance your complexion. Would it make a suitable wedding gown?''

"Yes, and it will remake a very fine evening dress, too. With careful cutting, I might even contrive an underskirt for another occasion.''

"Excellent work, Madame Nip-cheese. Could you not squeeze a pair of drapes for the blue saloon out of it as well? There are only two pairs of windows, each six feet tall.''

With a warning rattle of the doorknob, Mrs. Wickfield came into the room. One glance at the couple, with Alex's arm around Anne's waist, caused her to take a delighted step backward.

"Don't leave, Auntie—*Mama!*" Alex said, stepping toward her. "Come and protect your lovely daughter, before I take advantage of her. Does she not look ravishing in white crepe?'' He put his other arm around Mrs. Wickfield's shoulder and gave her cheek a peck. It was typical Penholme behavior.

Smiling at the two, Anne thought Alex's true nature had always been warmly affectionate, like the rest of his family. Circumstances had made him behave differently, but beneath that enforced aloofness, he represented the best of the Penholmes—their warmth and love, without that streak of recklessness.

"Trying to steal my beau, Mama?" she teased, and pulled his arm back. Alex smiled with satisfaction at this display of mock jealousy. "Find your own. Alex is taken."

"You see how she means to be!" the mother quizzed. "Jealous as a green cow. It was not to steal your beau I came. I wonder if Anglin has a brother. . . . Robin and the girls are waiting to congratulate you. I thought ten minutes long enough for lovemaking. I run a decent house here, I'll have you know. Besides, the tea is getting cold."

"Oh, well, in that case!" Alex exclaimed. "We don't want to be wasting good tea."

Regency presents the popular and prolific...

JOAN SMITH